Philip Lee Phillips, Appleton P. C. Griffin, Library of Congress

# List of Books Relating to Cuba

including references to collected works and periodicals

Philip Lee Phillips, Appleton P. C. Griffin,  Library of Congress

**List of Books Relating to Cuba**
*including references to collected works and periodicals*

ISBN/EAN: 9783337378318

Printed in Europe, USA, Canada, Australia, Japan

Cover: Foto ©Andreas Hilbeck / pixelio.de

More available books at **www.hansebooks.com**

# LIBRARY OF CONGRESS.

# LIST OF BOOKS RELATING TO CUBA

(INCLUDING REFERENCES TO COLLECTED WORKS AND PERIODICALS),

BY

## A. P. C. GRIFFIN,

ASSISTANT LIBRARIAN OF CONGRESS,

WITH

# BIBLIOGRAPHY OF MAPS,

BY

## P. LEE PHILLIPS,

SUPERINTENDENT MAPS AND CHARTS DEPARTMENT,
LIBRARY OF CONGRESS.

FEBRUARY 25, 1898.—Presented by Mr. WETMORE, referred to the Committee
on the Library, and ordered to be printed.

## WASHINGTON:
GOVERNMENT PRINTING OFFICE.
1898.

# LETTER OF TRANSMITTAL.

FEBRUARY 22, 1898.

SIR: I have the honor to inclose a report containing a list of all the works relative to the island of Cuba, as well as references to collated works and periodicals upon that subject now in the Library of Congress.

Also a bibliography of maps of Cuba now in the department of maps and charts.

The general interest felt in Cuban affairs will, it is believed, give this report special value.

The catalogue of books was prepared by A. P. C. Griffin; the bibliography of the maps by P. Lee Phillips, members of the library staff.

Yours, very truly,

JOHN RUSSELL YOUNG,
*Librarian of Congress.*

Hon. GEORGE P. WETMORE,
*Chairman of the Joint Committee on the Library,*
*United States Senate, Washington, D. C.*

3

# INTRODUCTION.

In the composition of this list it has not been the purpose to include works upon the discovery and occupation of Cuba in the fifteenth and sixteenth centuries. That belongs to the history of maritime exploration. It has been the aim to bring out the works treating of the political history as it has affected this country, not, however, overlooking the natural history and resources of the island. The earliest political history recorded is that of Arrate's, which covers the period from the discovery to the year 1761, written in that year, but not published until 1830. It is a work of more than ordinary significance, as it treats particularly of the geographical and strategic importance of the capital of Cuba. The first political event treated in which the American colonies came into relations with the island is that of Lord Vernon's expedition in 1741, whose forces were reinforced by soldiers from Virginia and New York and other colonies. The capture of Havana in 1762 by the English with colonial volunteers is amply treated in Mante's History of the Late War in America, while we have personal narratives in two works: An Authentic Narrative, etc., by an officer; and Mackellar's Journal of the Landing of His Majesty's Forces on the Island of Cuba. The Journal of the Rev. John Graham, showing how the Provincial Soldiers Perished before Havana, was published by the Society of Colonial Wars at New York, and is reprinted in Halstead's Cuba.

The manuscript collections of this library contain the Vernon-Wager and other papers, which have many contemporary documents and narratives relative to the British designs against Cuba at this period. Dr. Friedenwald, the superintendent of manuscripts department, has made a synoptical list of the significant papers, which is printed as an appendix to this bibliography.

A primary source of information upon the political relations of the United States and Cuba is Wharton's Digest of International Law, which considers the subject in sections headed "Boundary of territorial waters" (S. 327); "Claims against Cuba for illegal arrests and embargoes" (S. 230); "Exactions in Cuba as to passports" (S. 191); "Extent of territorial waters" (S. 32); "Relations of the United States to Cuba" (S. 60); "Intercessions for prisoners in Cuba" (S. 52); "Policy of acquisition by United States" (S. 72); "Undue discriminations of justice in Cuba" (S. 230); "Cuban insurrections" (S. 60, 402);

"Claims for maltreatment of citizens of the United States" (S. 189); "Exactions by port laws" (S. 37). Wheaton's International Law also has expositions of incidents on such of our Cuban relations as involve questions coming within its scope. Cluskey's Political Text-Book contains the "Ostend manifesto" and President Fillmore's message against filibusters. Williams's Statesman's Manual gives the messages of the Presidents from Washington to Buchanan, and Richardson's compilation includes all down to the Administration of Johnson

The subject of our Cuban relations naturally comes in for full consideration in Curtis's Constitutional History of the United States, and in Von Holst's Constitutional and Political History of the United States. Rhodes's History of the United States, in vol. 1, pp. 316–321, considers "Slavery in Cuba;" vol. 1, pp. 393–396, "Buchanan on Cuba;" vol. 2, pp. 10–38. "Attempt to acquire Cuba;" vol. 2, pp. 10–38, "Marcy's part in the attempt to acquire Cuba." Henry Adams, in his History of the United States, vol. 5, p. 39, has a reference to "Madison on Cuba." Jefferson's attitude toward Cuba is considered in the same work, vol. 4, pp. 340–341. (See further, on this, Jefferson's Works, vol. 5, p. 444; vol. 7, pp. 288, 289.)

In Adams's Life of Gallatin is found a reference, p. 104, "Spain's conduct toward Americans in 1793;" in Gallatin's Writings, edited by Adams, "Danger of Great Britain taking possession," Letters to Jefferson, May 10, 1808; "The Cuban question, letter, December 22, 1820; letter concerning a rumored attack of United States on Cuba," December 30, 1826; "The United States' interest in Cuba," February 2, 1827.

The Panama mission and Canning's project as they relate to Cuba are illustrated in the Memoirs of John Quincy Adams, vol. 7, p. 177, et seq.; in Webster's Works, vol. 3, pp. 207–211 (declaration respecting Cuba, in speech April 14, 1821).

Calhoun's speech on the acquisition of Cuba, May 15, 1848, is printed in his works, vol. 4, pp. 449–469. Webster's Works, vol. 6, pp. 513–517, contain his letter to Mr. Barringer, minister to Spain, on the Lopez expedition; vol. 6, pp. 518–530, letters on the case of Thrasher; vol. 6, pp. 508–510, letter, November 13, 1851, to Calderon de la Barca on the execution of Americans at Havana; "Fillmore and the filibusters under Lopez" is a reference in Sargent's Political Man and Events, vol. 2, pp. 680–681. Curtis's Life of Buchanan (vol. 2, pp. 136–141) gives an account of Buchanan's action in regard to Cuba. Seward's Works, vol. 4, p. 61, contains his speech on the bill providing for the acquisition of Cuba. Sumner's speech, September 22, 1869, considering the question of recognition of Cuban belligerency, is printed in his works, vol. 13. In the list of books now presented there are included a few not in the Library. These last consist of some works in the library of the Department of State and a few which belonged to the late W. Hallett Phillips, esq., and now in the possession of his brother, P. Lee Phillips, esq.

# CUBA.

## BOOKS RELATING TO CUBA.

Abbot, Abiel. Letters written in the interior of Cuba, between the mountains of Arcana, to the east, and of Cusco, to the west, in the months of February, March, April, and May, 1828.
*Boston, 1829. 256 pp. 8º.*

Abbott, John S. C. South and North, or impressions received during a trip to Cuba and the South.
*New York, 1860. 352 pp. 12º.*
    Pages 38–61 deal with Cuba.

Acosta y Albear, Francisco de. Compendio historico del pasado y presente de Cuba y de su guerra insurreccional hasta el 11 de Marzo de 1875, con algunas apreciaciones relativas á su porvenir, por el brigadier D. Francisco de Acosta y Albear.
*Madrid, 1875. 100 pp. 8º.*                                *State Department.*

Aguilera, Francisco V., and Cespedes, Ramón. Notes about Cuba. Slavery. I—African slave trade. II—Abolition of slavery. III—Inferences from the last Presidential message. The Revolution. IV—Forces employed by Spain against Cuba. V—Condition of the Revolution. VI—Spanish anarchy in Cuba. VII—Conclusion.
*[New York, 1872.] 54 pp. 8º.*

[Aldama, Miguel de.] Cuba before the United States. Remarks on the Hon. Charles Sumner's speech, delivered at the Republican convention of Massachusetts, the 22d September, 1869. Adopted and approved by the Central Republican Junta of Cuba and Porto Rico.
*New York, 1869. 39 pp. 8º.*
    On the slavery question as affecting the Cuban cause in United States.

[Aldama, Miguel de, and Echeverria, José Antonio.] Facts about Cuba. Published under authority of the New York Cuban Junta.
*New York, 1870. 31 pp. 8º.*

[———] Facts about Cuba. To the Congress of the United States of America now assembled. January, 1875.
*New York, 1875. 36 pp. 8º.*                                *State Department.*
    Pages 33–36 contain "Constitution of the Republic of Cuba," 1869.

Alexander, *Sir* James Edward. Transatlantic sketches, comprising visits to the most interesting scenes in North and South America, and the West Indies. In two volumes.
*London, 1833. Illustrated. 8º.*
    Volume 1. pages 315–369 contain an interesting account of Cuba, its people, statistics, etc.

**Ampère**, Jean Jacques Antoine. Promónade en Amérique, États-Unis—Cuba—Mexique.
    *Paris, 1855. 2 vols. 8°.*

**Andueza**, José María de. Isla de Cuba pintoresca, histórica, política, literaria, mercantil ó industrial. Recuerdos, apuntes, impresiones de dos épocas.
    *Madrid, 1841. 182 pp. Plates L.8°.*

**[Arango**, José de.] Nadie se asuste por la segunda y última esplicación mia sorbe [*sic*] la independencia de la Isla de Cuba.
    *Habana, 1821. 42 pp. sm. 4°.*

**[Armas y Cespedes**, J. de.] Position of the United States on the Cuban question.
    *New York, 1872. 20 pp. 8°.*                                 *Phillips.*

**Arrate**, José Martin Felix de. Llave del nuevo mundo antemural de las Indias occidentales. La Habana descripta: noticias de su fundacion, aumentos y estado. Compuesta por D. José Martin Felix de Arrate, natural y regidor perpetuo de dicha ciudad.
    *Habana, 1830. (4), xvi, 274 pp. 8°.*

> The first xvi pages are taken up with an introduction by the Real Sociedad patriótica de amigos del pais, under whose auspices the work was published. Arrate's history was written in 1761 but remained in manuscript until its publication by the above-named society as "cuadernos 1–4 of a projected series entitled 'Materiales relativos á la historia de Cuba.'" The title is an allusion to the important geographical and strategetical situation of the capital of Cuba.
> Reviewed in Amer. Q. Rev. Vol. 10, p. 230.

**Aubertin**, J. J. A flight with distances. The States, the Hawaiian Islands, Canada, British Columbia, Cuba, the Bahamas.
    *London, 1888. viii, (2), 352 pp. Illus. 2 maps. 8°.*
> Pages 333–345 describe a visit to Havana. Unimportant.

**An authentic journal** of the siege of the Havana. By an Officer. To which is prefixed, a plan of the siege of the Havana, showing the landing, encampments, approaches, and batteries of the English army. With the attacks and stations of the fleet.
    *London, printed for T. Jefferys, MDCCLXII. 44 pp. 8°.*

**Badeau**, Adam. Suggestions for a commercial treaty with Spain, with especial reference to Cuba.
    *[Jamaica, L. I., 1884.] 56 pp. 8°.*                                  *Phillips.*

**Baird**, Robert. Impressions and experiences of the West Indies and North America in 1849.
    *Philadelphia, 1850. 354 pp. 12°.*
> Pages 99–132 are devoted to Cuba. Touches on the question of acquisition by the United States.

**Baker**, Frank Collins. A naturalist in Mexico, being a visit to Cuba, Northern Yucatan, and Mexico. With maps and illustrations.
    *Chicago, 1895. 145 pp. 8°.*

**Ballou**, Maturin Murray. History of Cuba; or, notes of a traveller in the Tropics. Being a political, historical, and statistical account of the island, from the first discovery to the present time. Illustrated.
    *Boston, 1854. 230 pp. 8°.*

**Bas y Cortes**, Vicente. Cartas al rey acerca de la isla de Cuba.
    *Havana, 1871. xiii, 237 pp. 8°.*

**Beauvallet**, Léon. Rachel and the new world. A trip to the United States and Cuba. Translated from the French of Léon Beauvallet.
*New York, 1856. xiv, 404 pp. 16°.*
Pages 319-370. On "The Queen of the Antilles."

**Benjamin**, Judah Philip. Speech on the acquisition of Cuba. Delivered in the United States Senate, Friday, February 11, 1859.
[*Washington, 1859.*] *16 pp. 8°.* *Phillips.*
No title page. Half title. Favorable to purchase of Cuba.

**Benoist**, Charles. L'Espagne, Cuba et les États-Unis.
*Paris, 1898. xvii, (1), 269 pp. 12°.*
Reprinted from Revue des deux mondes, May, June, 1894, Oct., Nov., 1897.

[**Betancourt**, José Ramón.] Las dos banderas. Apuntes históricos sobre la insurrección de Cuba. Cartas al excmo. Sr. Ministro de ultramar. Soluciones para Cuba.
*Sevilla, 1870. 197 pp. 8°.*

**Bloomfield**, J. H. A Cuban expedition.
*London, 1896. 296 pp. 8°.*

**Bonnycastle**, Richard Henry. Spanish America; or a descriptive, historical, and geographical account of the dominions of Spain in the Western hemisphere . . . Illustrated by a map of . . . the West India islands and an engraving, representing the comparative altitudes of the mountains in those regions.
*Philadelphia, 1849. 488 pp. 8°.*
Pages 141-147 relate to Cuba.

**The Book** of Blood. An authentic record of the policy adopted by modern Spain to put an end to the war for the independence of Cuba. (October, 1868, to November 10, 1873.)
*New York: (N. Ponce de Leon, translator and printer.) 1873. viii, 66 pp. 8°.*

**Brooks**, Edward P. Free trade with Cuba. The Cuban question commercially and politically considered. An argument in behalf of the new republic by Ed. P. Brooks.
*Washington, D. C., 1869. 20 pp. 8°.*

**Brownson**, Orestes Augustus. Opiniones de un anglo-americano acerca de la expedicion cubana y los anexionistas. Traducido del Brownson's Quarterly Review correspondiente al mes de Octobre del 1850. Por. E. J. G.
*Nueva Orleans, Diciembre 1850. 64 pp. 16°.*
Denounces the Lopez expedition.

**Bureau of American Republics.** Bulletin No. 10, July, 1891. Import duties of Cuba and Puerto Rico.
*Washington, 1891. v, (1), 114 pp. 8°.*

**Cabrera**, Raimundo. Cuba y sus jueces (rectificaciones oportunas).
*Habana, 1887. 281, (1), 31, (2) pp. 8°.*

—— *Same.* 7a edicion ilustrada y aumentada con notas y un apendice.
*Filadelfia, 1891. 333 pp. 8°.*
A reply to F. Moreno's "Cuba y su gente."

—— Cuba and the Cubans. Translated from the 8th Spanish edition of "Cuba y sus jueces," by Laura Guitéras. Revised and edited by Louis Edward Levy.
*Philadelphia, 1896. Illustrated. 442 pp. Folded map. 8°.*

**Campbell, Rean.** Around the corner to Cuba.
>*1889. N. Y. 46 pp. Colored views. 3 folded maps. sm. 4°.*

**Castillo, Cárlos del.** Carta de Cárlos del Castillo al director de "La Independencia" (de Nueva York), respondiendo á su artículo editorial del 28 de Agosto de 1874, titulado "Digamos algo sobre nuestros asuntos."
>*London, 1874. 28 pp. 16°.*           *State Department.*

**[Cattell, Alexander Gilmore, jr.]** To Cuba and back in twenty-two days. A. G. C., jr.
>*Philadelphia, 1874. 47 pp. 12°.*

**Chester, Greville John.** Transatlantic sketches in the East Indies, South America, Canada, and the United States.
>*London, 1869. xvi, 405 pp. 8°.*
>>Pages 172-190 describe Cuba.

**Cisneros, Evángeline.** The story of Evangeline Cisneros. Told by herself.
>*N. Y. Continental publishing co. 1898.*

**Clark, James Hyde.** Cuba and the fight for freedom. A powerful and thrilling history of the "Queen of the Antilles," the oppression of the Spanish government, the insurrection of 1868 and the compromise of 1878, and a full and vivid account of the present struggle of the people for liberty and independence. Profusely illustrated.
>*Philadelphia, [1896]. 512 pp. 8°.*

**Claviac, José.** Estadística general de enfermos asistidos en los hospitales y enfermerías militares de la isla de Cuba durante la campaña, 1° Nov. 1868 á fin de Junio 1878.
>*(In Pan-American Medical Congress. Trans. Pt. 1, pp. 767-769. Washington, 1895.)*

**Concha, José Gutierrez de la,** *Marqués de la Habana.* Memorias sobre el estado político, gobierno y administracion de la isla de Cuba. Por el teniente General Don José de la Concha.
>*Madrid, 1853. ix, (1), 362, 41, (2) pp. Folded map. 8°.*

—— Memoria sobre la guerra de la isla de Cuba y sobre su estado político y económico, desde abril de 1874 hasta marzo de 1875. Por el Capitan General de ejército Marqués de la Habana.
>*Madrid, 1875. 179 pp. Folded map. 8°.*

**Correa, Diego.** El ciudadano Don Diego Correa al excmo. sr. Capitan General, gefe superior político, &c. Cuarta edición.
>*Habana. 1822. 13 pp. 8°.*

**Correspondence** on the proposed tripartite convention relative to Cuba.
>*Boston: Little, Brown and Company. 1853. 64 pp. 8°.*
>>Contains message from the President, Millard Fillmore, communicating a report from the Secretary of State, Edward Everett, with the following papers:
>>Letter of the Count de Sartiges to Mr. Webster, April 23, 1852; M. de Turgot au Comte de Sartiges (letter of instructions), Mar. 31, 1852; Project of the proposed convention; Letter from John F. Crampton to Mr. Webster, April 23, 1852; Letter of instructions of the Earl of Malmesbury to Mr. Crampton, April 8, 1852; Draught of convention; Mr. Webster to the Count de Sartiges, April 29, 1852; The Count de Sartiges to Mr. Webster, July 8, 1852; Mr. Crampton to Mr. Webster, July 8, 1852; Mr. Everett to the Count de Sartiges, Dec. 1, 1852.
>>Appendix.—Answer of Lord Russell to Mr. Everett's letter on the proposed tripartite treaty, Feb. 16, 1853; John F. Crampton to the Earl of Clarendon, April 18, 1853; Letters from Edward Everett to Lord John Russell, Sept. 17, 1853.
>>    \*     \*     \*     \*     \*
>>NOTE.—Wharton, in his Digest of International Law, referring to the writings of

Mr. Everett, here printed, says "that for wisdom and eloquence they are unexcelled by any papers that have ever issued from the State Department; and that they maintain an exposition of our true policy as to territorial accretion, which for its statesmanlike power, its nonpartisan broadness of base, as well as for its attractiveness of style, peculiarly fit it to be one of the standards to which political authorities of the future should appeal."

**Costales, Manuel.** Elogio del Dr. D. Tomás Romay, médico honorario de la Real cámara.
*Habana, 1850. 14 pp. Portrait. 8°.*

**Cuadro** estadístico de la siempre fiel isla de Cuba, correspondiente al año de 1846, formado bajo la dirección y protección del excmo sr. gobernador y Capitan General Don. Leopoldo O-Donnell por una Comision de oficiales y empleados particulares.
*Habana, 1847. vii, (3), 266, 44, (1) pp. 4°.*

**Cuba.** An appeal from the Board of Planters and the Merchants of Havana, addressed to Alfonso XII.
*New York, 1879. 15 pp. 8°.*        *State Department.*

—— Bando de gobernacion y policia de la Isla de Cuba, expedido por el excmo. Sr. D. Gerónimo Valdes, Presidente Gobernador y Capitan General. Segunda edicion.
*Habana, 1844. 124, vii, (2), 34, (1) pp. 8°.*

—— Constitution of the Republic of Cuba. Adopted by the constitutional convention, and unanimously approved by the Cuban Congress assembled at Guiamaro, the provisional capital of the Republic, on the 10th day of April, 1869, and the first of the independence of Cuba.
*New York, [1869.] (3) pp. 4°.*

**Cuba and the United States.** Some pertinent facts concerning the struggle for independence. By the Cuban delegation in Atlanta.
*Atlanta, 1897. 24 pp. 8°.*

**Cuba before the United States.** Remarks on the Hon. Charles Sumner's speech, delivered at the Republican convention of Massachusetts, the 22d September, 1869.
*New York, 1869. 39 pp. 8°.*

**Cuba.** Fragments of a letter addressed to a distinguished party, in May, 1869, with notes and appendix. Also, report of Marshal Serrano, Duke de la Torre, (present regent of Spain) on the interrogatories submitted to him by the Spanish Government in the matter of reform in the régime of the Antilles. Translated from the Spanish.
*New York, 1869. 25 pp. 8°.*       *Phillips.*

**Cuba y America.** Periodico quincenal. Nos. 10—18. Agosto 15—Dec. 15, 1897.
*New York, 1897. 8 nos.*

**Cuban League.** The present condition of affairs in Cuba. A report of a special committee of the Cuban League of the United States. Submitted and adopted by the Executive Committee of the league. August 23, 1877.
*New York, 1877. 16 pp. 8°.*

**Cuban question, The,** and American policy in the light of common sense.
*New York, 1869. 39 pp. Folded map. 8°.*

**Cuban question, The,** in England. Extracts from opinions of the press.
*Printed by Read, Hole & Co., London (1871). 19, (1), 3 pp. 8°.*     *Phillips.*

**Cuyas,** Arturo, *and others.* The new constitutional laws for Cuba. Text of the recent measures for the self-government of the island, with comments thereon. Also a brief review of the evolution of Spanish colonization, and a statistical comparison of the progress of Cuba under Spanish rule with that of independent Spanish-American countries.
*New York, 1897. 168 pp. 8°.*

> Consists of three articles: By Arturo Cuyas, Antonia Cuyas, L. V. Abad de Las Casas, presenting the text of the reform law of 1895, with expository comments, constituting a justification of the Spanish policy.

**Dana,** Richard Henry, Jr. To Cuba and back. A vacation voyage.
*Boston, 1859. 288 pp. 12°.*
—— *Same. London, 1859. 256 pp. 8°.*
—— *Same. Boston, [1887]. 288 pp. 12°.*

**Davis,** Reuben. Speech on his resolutions for the acquisition of Cuba. Delivered in the House of Representatives, January 31, 1859.
*Washington; printed by Lemuel Towers, 1859. 15 pp. 8°.*        *Phillips.*

**Davis,** Richard Harding. Cuba in war time. Illustrated by Frederick Remington.
*New York, 1897. 143 pp. 12°.*

—— A year from a correspondent's note-book. Illustrated.
*London and New York, 1898 (1897). 305 pp. Portrait. 8°.*

> Pages 97–133 contain "Cuba in war time."

**Demoticus Philalethes,** *pseud.* Yankee travels through the island of Cuba; or, the men and government, the laws and customs of Cuba, as seen by American eyes. By Demoticus Philalethes.
*New York, 1856. xii, ix, 412 pp. 12°.*

**[Dominguez,** Firmin Valdes]. Los voluntarios de la Habana en el acontecimiento de los estudiantes de medicina, por uno de ellos condenado á seis años de presidio.
*Madrid, 1873. 148, (1) pp. Portraits. Plates. 8°.*

> First Edition of "El 27 de Noviembre de 1871."
> Bound with [Betancourt, José R.] "Las dos banderas."

—— El 27 de Noviembre de 1871. 2ª edicion.
*Habana, 1887. 270, (1) pp. 8°.*

> An enlarged edition of the preceding.

**Draper,** William Francis. Against the recognition of belligerent rights in Cuba under present conditions. Speech in the House, March 2, 1896.
*Washington, 1896. 7 pp. 8°.*

**España y Cuba.**
[*Paris, 1876.*] *37 pp. 8°.*        *State Department.*
No title page. Half title.

**Fernandez de Castro,** Manuel. Estudio sobre las minas de oro de la isla de Cuba, y muy particularmente sobre la de San Blas de las Meloneras en el Partido de Guaracabuya, jurisdicion de Remedios.
*Habana, 1864. 104 pp. 8°.*

**Ferrer,** Miguel Rodriguez. Los nuevos peligros de Cuba entre sus cinco crisis actuales, por Miguel Rodriguez Ferrer, jefe de administracion y propietario en Cuba.
*Madrid, 1862. 197 pp. 16°.*

**Ferrer de Couto**, José. Cuba may become independent. A political pamphlet bearing upon current events. Translated from the Spanish by Charles Kirchhoff.
New York, 1872. 142 pp. 8°.
Presentation copy to Caleb Cushing, with author's autograph on fly-leaf.

**Fisher**, Richard Swainson. The Spanish West Indies, Cuba and Porto Rico; geographical, political, and industrial Cuba; from the Spanish of Don J. M. de la Torre. Porto Rico: by J. T. O'Neil. Edited by Richard S. Fisher, M. D. Illustrated by a new and accurate map.
New York, 1861. 190 pp. 12°.

**Ford**, Isaac N. Tropical America.
New York, 1893. x, (4), 409 pp. Photogravures. Folded Map. 8°.
Pages 260-290 contain "The Last Spanish Stronghold."

**Froude**, James Anthony. The English in the West Indies; or, the bow of Ulysses. With illustrations engraved on wood by G. Pearson, after drawings by the author.
New York, 1888. x, (3), 373 pp. 8°.
Pages 288-349 deal with Cuba.

**Facts about Cuba.** Published under authority of the New York Cuban Junta.
New York, 1870. 31 pp. 8°.

**Galino**, Dioniso Alcalo. Cuba en 1858.
Madrid, 1859. 254 pp. 8°.

**Gallenga**, Antonio. The Pearl of the Antilles.
London, 1873. (4), 202 pp. 8°.
Favorable to Spain.

**Garcia Verdago**, Vicente. Cuba contra España. Apuntes para la historia de la rebelion de la isla de Cuba, que principió el 10 de Octubre de 1868.
Madrid, 1869. 422 pp. 8°.

**Gibbes**, Robert Wilson. Cuba for invalids.
New York, 1860. xii, 214 pp. 12°.

**Gonzalez de los Rios**, Pelayo. Ensayo histórico-estadístico de la instruccion pública de la isla de Cuba. O breve reseña de sus adelantos, de su estado actual y de su reforma, particularmente de la instruccion primaria, precedido de varios estudios sobre enseñanza.
Habana, 1865. L. 8°.
Extract from Memorias de la Real sociedad económica y anales de fomento.

**Goodman**, Walter. The Pearl of the Antilles, or an artist in Cuba.
London, 1873. xiv, 304 pp. 8°.

**Granier de Cassagnac**, A. Voyage aux Antilles françaises, anglaises, danoises, espagnoles à Saint-Domingue et aux États-Unis d'Amérique.
Paris, 1844. 2 vols. 8°.
Volume 2, pages 349-368 are devoted to an account of the resources, etc., of Cuba.

**Guitéras**, John, editor. Free Cuba, her oppressions, struggle for liberty, history, and present condition, with the causes and justification of the present war for independence, by Rafael M. Merchán, one of the leaders of the Cuban patriots. The history of the war, by Gonzalo de Quesada, Cuban chargé d'affaires at Washington, and special chapters by F. G. Pierra, chairman of the revolutionary committee of the United States, and by Capt. Ricardo J. Navarro, of the Cuban army. Edited by Dr. John Guitéras, of the University of Pennsylvania.
[Philadelphia.] Publishers' Union, 1896. 617 pp. Illustrated. 12°.

**Guitéras,** Pedro J.　Historia de la isla de Cuba.　Con notas ó ilustraciones.
　　*New York, 1865.　2 vols.　8º.*

**Gundlach,** Juan.　Contribución á la mamalogia cubana.
　　*Habana, 1877.　8º.*
—— Contribución á la fauna malacologia cubana.
　　*Habana, 1878.　8º.*
—— Contribución á la entomologia cubana.
　　*Habana, 1881.　8º.*
—— Contribución á la erpetologia cubana.
　　*Habana, 1880.　8º.*

**Hardy,** W.　The history and adventures of the Cuban expedition, from the first
　　movement down to the dispersion of the army at Key West, and the arrest
　　of General Lopez; also, an account of the ten deserters at Isla de Mugeres.
　　By Lieutenant Hardy, of the Kentucky battalion.
　　*Cincinnati, 1850.　94 pp.　8º.*

**Hazard,** Samuel.　Cuba with pen and pencil.
　　*Hartford, 1871.　584 pp.　Woodcuts.　8º.*

**[Hernandez,** Jacinto.]　Cuba por dentro.
　　*N. P. (187-).　54 pp.　8º.*
　　　　Bound with [Betancourt, J. R.] "Las dos banderas."

**Herrero,** Miguel Blanco.　Isla de Cuba.　Su situacion actual y reformas que reclama.
　　*Madrid, 1876.　86, (1) pp.　8º.*

**Howe,** Julia Ward.　A trip to Cuba.
　　*Boston, 1860.　iv, 251 pp.　12º.*
　　　　A reprint of articles published in the Atlantic Monthly, May–November, 1859.

**Huber,** B.　Aperçu statistique de l'île de Cuba, précédé de quelques lettres sur la
　　Havane, et suivi de tableaux synoptiques, d'une carte de l'île, et du tracé
　　des côtes depuis la Havane jusqu'à Matanzas.
　　*À Paris, 1840.　326, (2) pp.　6 folded sheets.　8º.*

**Humboldt,** Friedrich Heinrich Alexander *Freiherr* von.　Ensayo político sobre la
　　isla de Cuba, por el Baron A. de Humboldt, con un mapa; obra traducida
　　al castellano por D. José Lopez de Bustamente.　Nueva edicion.
　　*Paris, 1840.　xxxii, 361, (3) pp.　8º.*

—— The island of Cuba, by Alexander Humboldt.　Translated from the Spanish
　　with notes and a preliminary essay.　By J. S. Thrasher.
　　*New York, 1856.　397 pp.　Folded map.　8º.*
　　　　The translator was for a long time prior to 1851 a resident of Cuba, from which he was
　　　　banished in consequence of the political sentiments of a paper which he published.
　　　　He was a leading man of the organization of the filibustering expedition under
　　　　Quitman.

—— Voyage de Humboldt et Bonpland.　6ᵉ partie, botanique.　Plantes équi-
　　noxiales, recueillies au Mexique dans l'île de Cuba.
　　*Paris, 1808-1809.　2 vols.　Plates Fº.*

—— Personal narrative of travels to the equinoctial regions of the new continent,
　　during the years 1799-1804.　Translated by Helen Maria Williams.
　　*London, 1829.　7 vols.　8º.*
　　　　Volume 7, pages 1-370 contain "Political essay on the island of Cuba," translated from
　　　　the following work.

**Humboldt,** Friedrich Heinrich Alexander *Freiherr* von. Voyages aux régions équinoxiales du nouveau continent, fait en 1799, 1800, 1801, 1802, 1803, et 1804, par Al. de Humboldt et A. Bonpland; rédigé pa Alexandre de Humboldt. Avec deux atlas (Relation historique).
*Paris, 1825. 4 vols. 4°. Atlas 2 vols. F°.*

> Volume 3, pages 345-483 contain Humboldt's Essai politique sur l'isle de Cuba.

**Hurlbut,** William Henry. Gan-Eden: or, Pictures of Cuba.
*Boston, 1854. viii, (4), 235 pp. 12°.*

**Jackson,** Julia Newell. A winter holiday in summer lands.
*Chicago, 1890. 221 pp. Woodcuts. 12°.*

**Jones,** Alexander. Cuba in 1851; containing authentic statistics of the population, agriculture and commerce of the island for a series of years, with official and other documents in relation to the revolutionary movements of 1850 and 1851.
*New York, 1851. 80 pp. 2 maps. Portrait of Lopez. 8°.*

**[Kenney,** Edward.] Report of our mission in Cuba. October, 1874–October, 1877.
*Detroit, 1878. 15 pp. 8°.*                                     *State Department.*

> On the work of a mission organized by the House of Bishops of the United States

**[Kimball,** Richard Burleigh.] Cuba and the Cubans; comprising a history of the island of Cuba, its present social, political, and domestic condition; also, its relation to England and the United States. By the author of "Letters from Cuba." With an appendix, containing important statistics, and a reply to Senor Saco on annexation. Translated from the Spanish.
*New York, 1850. 255 pp. 12°.*

**[Kingsley,** Vine Wright.] Spain, Cuba, and the United States. Recognition and the Monroe Doctrine. By Americus.
*New York, 1870. 34 pp. 8°.*

**Kirchner,** Adelaide Rosalind. A flag for Cuba. Pen sketches of a recent trip across the Gulf of Mexico to the island of Cuba. Illustrated with snap-shot views.
*New York (1897). x, 177 pp. 12°.*

**Latimer,** Elizabeth Wormley. Spain in the nineteenth century.
*Chicago, 1897. 441 pp. Portrait. 8°.*

> Pages 301-422 contain some observations on the Cuban question.

**Letters** from the Havana, during the year 1820: containing an account of the present state of the island of Cuba, and observations on the slave trade.
*London, 1821. viii, (2), 135 pp. Map. 8°.*

**Leon,** José Ruiz. Los filibusteros en Madrid y el apresamiento del "Virginius."
*Madrid, 1874. 97 pp. 8°.*                                     *State Department.*

**Llamiento** de la isla de Cuba á la nación española, dirigido al excmo. ó illmo. Señor Don Baldomero Espartero, duque de la Victoria, presidente del consejo de ministros, por un hacendado, en diciembre de 1854.
*New York [1856]. ir, 230, r, (1) pp. 8°.*

> Examines into the character and workings of the Spanish colonial system from a Cuban standpoint.

> *Reviewed by A. W. Ely in Bow's Review, vol. 18 (Feb., March, 1855), pp. 163-167, 305-311.*

**Lobé**, Guillaume. Cuba et les grandes puissances occidentales de l'Europe ou identité qui existe entre les intérêts et l'importance actuels et futurs de l'île de Cuba, à l'égard du nouveau monde, et en particulier des États-Unis de l'Amérique septentrionale. Collection de brochures et de lettres adressées à Madrid sur ces objets vitaux.
> *Paris, 1856. 220 pp. 8°.*

**Luz**, José de la. Informe presentado á la Real junta de fomento de agricultura . . . de esta isla, 11 de diciembre de 1833 en el espediente sobre traslacion, reforma y ampliacion de la escuela náutica en el pueblo de Regla.
> *Habana, 1834. (4), iii, (1), 151, (3) pp. 4°.*

**[Macias**, Juan Manuel.] Cuba in revolution; a statement of facts.
> *London, printed by Head, Hole & Co. 1871. 40, (1) pp. 8°.*
>> "The undersigned, acting in the name of the Republican Government of that Island, presents to the public the following plain statement of the causes which provoked and justified the uprising of the Cuban people." *Preface.*      *Phillips.*

———— *editor.* The Cuban question in the Spanish Parliament. (Debate in the Cortes.) Extracts from speeches made by Señores Diaz Quintero, Benot, Salmeron, Sanroma, Garrido, Labra, Orense, and others.
> *London, 1872. 32 pp. 8°.*      *State Department.*

**Mackellar**, Patrick. A correct journal of the landing his majesty's forces on the island of Cuba; and of the siege and surrender of the Havannah, August 13, 1762. By Patrick Mackellar, Chief Engineer. Published by authority. The Second edition.
> *London, printed. Boston, reprinted 1762. 19 pp. 8°.*

**Madden**, Richard Robert. The island of Cuba: its resources, progress, and prospects considered in relation especially to the influence of its prosperity on the interest of the British West India colonies.
> *London, 1853. xxiv, 252 pp. 12°.*

**Mahan**, Alfred Thayer The interest of America in sea power, present and future.
> *Boston, 1897. vi, (4), 304 pp. 8°.*
>> Treats of the naval importance of Cuba.

**Mallory**, Stephen Russell. Speech on the Cuba bill, delivered in the Senate of the United States February [24], 1859.
> *Baltimore—Printed by John Murphy, 1859. 32 pp. 8°.*

**Marmier**, Xavier. Lettres sur l'Amérique. Canada—États-Unis—Havane—Rio de La Plata.
> *Paris, [1851]. 2 vols. 16°.*
>> Volume 2, pages 1-96 treat of Cuba, its political and social condition.

**Massé**, Étienne Michel. L'île de Cuba et la Havane, ou histoire, topographie, statistique, mœurs, usages, commerce et situation politique de cette colonie, d'après un journal écrit sur les lieux. Par E. M. Massé.
> *Paris, 1825. 407, (3) pp. 8°.*

**Merchan**, Rafael M. *See* Guitéras, John, *editor.* Free Cuba.

**Merlin**, María de los Mercédis de Jaruco, *comtesse.* La Havane, par Madame la comtesse Merlin.
> *Paris, 1844. 3 vols. 8°.*
>> The author was a native of Cuba.

**Mitjanes,** Aurelio. Estudio sobre el movimiento cientifico y literaria de Cuba. Obra postuma publicada por suscrición popular.
*Habana, 1890. XXXI. 395 pp. 8°.*

**Montaos y Robillard,** Francisco. Proyecto de emancipacion de la esclavitud en la isla de Cuba, por el Coronel de caballeria.
*Madrid, 1865. 49 pp. 4°.*

**Moore,** Rachel Wilson. Journal kept during a tour to the West Indies and South America in 1863-64.
*Philadelphia, 1867. 274 pp. 12°.*

    Pages 21-58 describe a stay in Havana and the neighborhood.

**Murray,** Henry Anthony. Lands of the slave and the free, or Cuba, the United States, and Canada.
*London. G. Routledge. 1857. xxiii, 280 pp. 2 maps. 10 pls. (Woodcuts.) 12°.*

**New constitution** establishing self-government in the islands of Cuba and Porto Rico. Authorized translation of the preamble and royal decree of November 25, 1897, published in the Official Gazette of Madrid. With comments by Cuban autonomists on the scope of the plan and its liberality as compared with Canadian autonomy and Federal state rights. Published at the office of "Cuba."
*New York, 1898. 74, (1) pp. 16°.*

**[Nason, Daniel.]** A journal of a tour from Boston to Savannah, thence to Havana, in the Island of Cuba, with occasional notes during a short residence in each place. . . . By a Citizen of Cambridgeport.
*Cambridge, 1849. 114 pp. 16°.*

**Norman,** Benjamin Moore. Rambles by land and water, or notes of travel in Cuba and Mexico; including a canoe voyage up the river Panuco, and researches among the ruins of Tamaulipas, etc.
*New York, 1845. 216 pp. Plates. Woodcuts in the text. 12°.*

**Norton,** Francis L. Cuba. (Letters to Clarles Sumner.)
*New York, Dec. 16th, 1873. 15 pp. 8°.*

**O., O. D. D.** The history of the late expedition to Cuba, by O. D. D. O., one of the participants, with an appendix, containing the last speech of the celebrated orator, S. S. Prentiss, in defense of Gen. Lopez.
*New Orleans, 1850. (2), 89 pp. 8°.*

**Ober,** Fred A. Under the Cuban flag, or the Cacique treasure. Illustrated.
*Boston, [1897]. 316 pp. 8°.*

**O'Kelly,** James J. The Mambi-land, or adventures of a Herald correspondent in Cuba.
*Philadelphia, 1874. 359 pp. Woodcut. 8°.*

**Ostend** manifesto, The. 1854.
*New York, 1892. (American history leaflets.)*

    The text of the Ostend manifesto is printed in Cluskey's political text-book, pages 435-438; in Macdonald's Select Documents illustrative of the history of the United States; Halstead's Cuba.

**Paseo** pintoresco por la isla de Cuba. Obra artística ó literaria en que se pintan y describen los edificios, los monumentos, los campos y las costumbres de este privilegiado suelo, publicado por los empresarios de la biografia del Gobierno y Capitania General.
*Habana, 1841-42. 2 vols. in 1. obl. 16°.*

    Most of the text is by Manuel Costales, A. Bachiller and C. Villaverde.

**Pezuela,** Jacob de la.  Diccionario geográfico, estadístico, histórico de la isla de Cuba.
*Madrid, 1863–66.  4 vols.  L. 8°.*

——  Historia de la isla de Cuba.
*Madrid, 1868.  2 vols.  8°.*

**Philippo,** James Mursell.  The United States and Cuba.
*London, 1857.  xi, (1), 476 pp.  8°.*

**Pichardo,** Estéban.  Geografía de la isla de Cuba, por Don Estéban Pichardo.  Abogado, secretario de la Comision de division territorial ó interino de la de estadística.  Publicase bajo los auspicios de la Real Junta de fomento.  1ª–3ª parte.
*Habana, 1854.  3 vols. in 1.  8°.*
Lacks the fourth part.

**Pierra,** Fidel G.  Cuba: Physical features of Cuba, her past, present, and possible future.  Published by the Cuban delegation in the United States.
*New York, 1896.  (2), 51, (2) pp.  Folded map.  8°.*

——  *See* GUITÉRAS, John, *editor.*  Free Cuba.

**Piñeyro,** Enrique.  Morales Lemus y la revolución de Cuba.  Estudio histórico.
*New York, 1871.  140 pp.  Facsimile.  12°.*          *State Department.*

**Piron,** Hippolyte.  L'ile de Cuba—Santiago—Puerto-Principe—Matanzas et la Havane.  Ouvrage orné de gravures dessinées par L. Bertou d'après des photographies.
*Paris, 1876.  (4), 325, (1) pp.  12°.*

**Prince,** John C.  Cuba illustrated with the biography and portrait of Christopher Columbus, containing also general information relating to Havana, Matanzas, Cienfuegos, and the Island of Cuba.  With illustrations and maps, together with an Anglo-Spanish vocabulary.  6th edition.
*New York [1894].  260 pp.  16°.*

[——]  Souvenir of the Island of Cuba.
*[New York.]  Copyright, 1894, by J. C. Prince.  (50) pp.  Photogravures.  obl. 16°.*

**Poey,** Felipe.  Geografía física y política de la isla de Cuba.  Edición 17a.
*Habana, 1857.  44 pp.  8°.*
——  Same.  Edición 18a.
*Habana, 1858.  44 pp.  8°.*

——  Memorias sobre la historia natural de la isla de Cuba, accompañadas de sumarios latinas y extractos en frances.
*Habana, 1851–58.  2 vols.  8°.*

**Quatrelles.**  Un parisien dans les Antilles—Saint-Thomas, Puerto-Rico, la Havane, la vie de province sous les tropiques.  Ouvrage illustré.
*Paris, 1897.*

**Quesada,** Gonzalo de.  History of the war.
*See* GUITÉRAS, John, *editor.*  Free Cuba.

**Quesada,** Manuel.  Address of Cuba to the United States.
*New York, 1873.  iv., 41 pp.  8°.*          *State Department.*

**Rawson,** James.  Cuba.  By Rev. James Rawson, A. M.
*New York, 1847.  70 pp.  Woodcuts.  16°.*

**Rea**, George Bronson. Facts and fakes about Cuba. A review of the various stories circulated in the United States concerning the present insurrection. By George Bronson Rea (field correspondent of "New York Herald"). Illustrated by William de La M. Cary.
*New York, 1897. 336 pp. 12°.*

**Robertson**, James. A few months in America; containing remarks on some of the industrial and commercial interests.
*London, [1855]. vii, 230 pp. 12°.*
   Pages 91–101 contain "Cuba; its annexation a gain or loss to the United States."

**Rosal y Vazquez de Mondragon**, Antonio del. Los mambíses. Memorias de un prisionero por el capitan de infautería Don Antonio del Rosal.
*Madrid, 1874. 44 pp. 8°.*
   Bound with [Betancourt, J. R.] "Las dos banderas."

**Rochas**, Victor de. Cuba under Spanish rule. By Dr. V. de Roches. From the "Revue contemporaine."
*New York (1869). 57 pp. 8°.*                                       *Phillips.*

**Routier**, Gaston. L'Espagne en.1897.
*Paris, 1897. Le Soudier.*
   "Devotes a large part of the book to Cuba and President McKinley's message."

**Rowan**, Andrew Summers, and Marathon Montrose **Ramsey**. The Island of Cuba. A descriptive and historical account of the Great Antilla.
*New York, 1896. x, 279 pp. 2 folded maps. 16°.*

**Sagra**, Ramón de la. Historia económico-política y estadística de la isla de Cuba ó sea de sus progresos en la poblacion, la agricultura, el comercio y las rentas.
*Habana, 1831. (4), xiii, (5), 386, (1) pp. 4°.*

—— Historia física, política y natural de la isla de Cuba.
*Paris, 1842-1851. 12 vols. Plates. F°.*
   Contents: 1ª parte—Historia física y politica: T. 1, Introduccion, geografía, clima, poblacion, agricultura. T. 2, Comercio, y gastos, fuerza armada. 2 vols. F°.
   2ª parte—T. 1, 2, Historia natural. T. 3, Mamiferos y aves. T. 4, Reptiles y peces. T. 5, Moluscos. T. 6, Fósiles. T. 7, Crustaceos, aragnides ó insectos. T. 8, Atlas de zoología. T. 9-11, Botánica. T. 12, Atlas de botánica.

—— Histoire physique, politique et naturelle de l'ile de Cuba. Poissons. Par A. Guichenot.
*Paris, 1853. (2), 206, (1) pp. 8°.*

—— Same. Mollusques. Par Alcide d'Orbigny.
*Paris, 1853. 2 vols. 8°.*
   This and the preceding work are translations from Sagra's *Historia física, etc.*

[**Santos Suarez**, Joaquin.] La cuestion Africana en la isla de Cuba, considerada bajo su doble aspecto de la trata interior y esterior. Par un cubano propietario.
*Madrid, 1863. 63 pp. 4°.*
   Bound with MONTAOS Y ROBILLARD Francisco. Proyecto de Emancipacion de la esclavitud en la isla de Cuba.

**Sedano**, Carlos de. Cuba. Estudios políticos por D. Carlos de Sedano, ex-diputado á Cortes.
*Madrid, 1872. (10), 3-457, (6) pp. 4°.*

**Serra Montalvo,** Rafael. Ensayo políticos. Segunda serie.
*New York, 1896. 221, (1), xri pp. Portrait. Sq. 16°.*
Mainly a reprint of newspaper articles advocating the Cuban cause. Contains a sketch of José Marti.

**Sirgado y Sequeira,** Pedro Pascual de. Elogio del Sr. Juan Manuel O'Farrill, pronunciado en la Real sociedad patriótica de la Habana.
*Habana, 1831. 14 pp. 8°.*

**Sivers,** Jegor von. Cuba, die Perle der Antillen. Reisenwürdigkeiten und Forschungen.
*Leipzig, 1861. ri, (2), 364 pp. 8°.*
Reviewed in The Nation, vol. 3 (Aug. 2, 1866), pp. 85–87.

**Smith,** Aaron. The atrocities of the pirates, or, a faithful narrative of the unparalleled sufferings endured by the author, during his captivity among the pirates of the Island of Cuba, with an account of the excesses and barbarities of those inhuman freebooters.
*London, 1824. ri, (1), 214 pp. 16°.*

———— *Same.* First American, from the London edition.
*New York, 1824. 158 pp. 16°.*

**Snow,** Freeman. Treaties and topics in American diplomacy.
*Boston, 1894. 8°.*
Pages 349–357 contain an outline history of the attempts made to acquire Cuba supposed to be favored by the United States government.

**Spain.** *Ministerio de ultramar.* Cuba desde 1850 á 1873. Coleccion de informes, memorias, proyectos y antecedentes sobre el gobierno de la isla de Cuba, relativos al citado período, que ha reunido por comision del gobierno D. Cárlos de Sedano y Cruzot, ex-diputado á Cortes.
*Madrid, imprenta nacional, 1873. 301, (3), 152, iv pp. F°.*

**Steele,** James W. Cuban sketches.
*New York, 1881. vii, (4), 220 pp. 12°.*

**Taylor,** John Glanville. The United States and Cuba: eight years of change and travel.
*London, 1851. xii, 328 pp. 12°.*

**Thrasher,** John S. A preliminary essay on the purchase of Cuba.
*New York, 1859. 95 pp. 12°.*

**Torre,** José Maria de la. Compendio de geografia física, política estadística y comparada de la isla de Cuba.
*Habana, 1854. ri, (3), 128 pp. 8°.*
Reviewed by A. W. Ely in De Bow's Review, vol. 17, p. 219, under the caption "Cuba as it is in 1854."

**Torronte,** Mariano. Bosquejo económico político de la isla de Cuba, comprensivo de varios proyectos de prudentes y saludables mejoras que pueden introducirse en su gobierno y administracion.
*Madrid, 1852–53. 2 vols. Portrait. 8°.*

———— Slavery in the island of Cuba, with remarks on the statements of the British press relative to the slave trade.
*London, 1853. 107, (1), 32 pp. 8°.*
The Spanish text and the English translation are printed on opposite pages. The last 32 pages consist of a translation of a pamphlet published at Madrid in 1841, entitled "Cuestion sobre la esclavitud en la isla de Cuba."

**Townshend,** Frederick Trench. Wild life in Florida, with a visit to Cuba.
London; 1875. xiv, 319 pp. Woodcut map. 8°.

Pages 168–217 describe Cuba.

**Trollope,** Anthony. The West Indies and the Spanish Main. Second edition.
London, 1860. iv, 395 pp. Map. 8°.

Pages 131–155 give an account of a visit to Cuba.

**Tucker,** George F. The Monroe doctrine.
Boston, 1885. 138 pp. 8°.

Cuba, pages 77–91.

**Tudor,** Henry. Narrative of a tour in North America; . . . with an excursion to
the Island of Cuba. In a series of letters, written in the years 1831–1832.
In two volumes.
London, 1834. 12°.

Volume 2, pages 97–136 describe a visit to Cuba.

**Turnbull,** David. Travels in the west. Cuba; with notices of Porto Rico and the
slave trade.
London, 1840. xvi, 574 pp. Map. 8°.

**[Tyng,** C. D.] The stranger in the Tropics: being a hand-book for Havana and
guide-book for travelers in Cuba, Puerto Rico, and St. Thomas. With de-
scriptions of the principal objects of interest; suggestions to invalids.
New York, 1868. 194 pp. Woodcut. Folded map. 16°.

**United States Government,** The, has injured the liberty of the people of Cuba.
The people of Cuba demand justice of the people of America.
[New York, 1849.] 24, 17 pp. Folded map. 8°.

Consists of extracts from "La Verdad," treating "of the advantages which the
annexation of Cuba offers to Americans, and in particular to the people of the United
States."

**Valiente,** Porfirio. Réformes dans les îles de Cuba et de Porto-Rico. Avec une
préface par Édouard Laboulaye.
Paris, 1869. xx, 412 pp. 8°.

**[Vernon,** Edward.] Original papers relating to the expedition to the Island of
Cuba.
London, printed for M. Cooper. MDCCXLIV. 219 pp. 8°.

**Vindicacion.** Cuestion de Cuba, por un Español Cubano.
Madrid, 1873. 85 pp. 8°.

Bound with [Betancourt, J. R.] "Las dos banderas."

**Vines,** Beñito. Investigaciones relativas á la circulacion ciclónica en los huracanes
de las Antillas.
Habana, 1895. 79 pp. 8°.

**Vives,** Francisco Dionisio. Relacion histórica de los beneficios hechos á la Real
sociedad económica, casa de beneficencia y demas dependencias de aquel
cuerpo. Habana, 1832. (4), 36, (1), pp. F°.

**Willis,** Nathaniel Parker. Health trip to the Tropics.
New York, 1853. 421, (1), xviii pp. 12°.

Pages 278–293 contain an account of visit to Havana.

**Wilson,** Thomas W. An authentic narrative of the piratical descents upon Cuba
made by hordes from the United States, headed by Narciso Lopez, a native
of South America; to which are added some interesting letters and decla-
rations from the prisoners, with a list of their names, etc.
Havana, September 1851. 44 pp. sm. 4°.

**Wilson**, Thomas W.   The Island of Cuba in 1850, being a description of the island, its resources, productions, commerce, &c.
*New Orleans, June 1850.   20 pp.   8°.*

[**Woodruff**, Julia Louisa Matilda.]   My winter in Cuba.   By W. M. L. Jay, author of "Shiloh."
*New York, 1871.   296 pp.   12°.*

[**Wurdiman**, F.]   Notes on Cuba, containing an account of its discovery and early history; a description of the face of the country, its population, resources, and wealth; its institutions and the manners and customs of its inhabitants.   With directions to travellers visiting the island.   By a Physician.
*Boston, 1844.   x, 359, (1), pp.   12°.*

**Zambrana**, Ramón.   Elogio del Señor Don Alejandro Ramirez, intendente de la Habana, leido á la Rl. sociedad económica.   .   .   .   13 de Diciembre de 1855.
*Habana, 1856.   14 pp.   8°.*

# ARTICLES IN MAGAZINES.

**1825.** Cuba without war. A. H. Everett.
*Scribners, 11 (April 1876), 376.*

**1829.** Cuba. The physical, statistical, and political features.
*Southern Review, vol. 4 (Nov. 1829), 285–321.*
Review of Humboldt's Essai politiqui; Huber's Aperçu; Sagra's Anales, 1827-29.

**1829.** Cuba. Review of Abbot's Letters. By W. Phillips.
*Christian Examiner, vol. 6 (May 1829), 259; North American Review, vol. 29
(July 1829), 199.*

**1829.** Political and statistical account of Cuba, Humboldt's.
*For. quarterly, vol. 3 (Jan. 1829), 400; Museum of Foreign Literature, vol. 14
(May 1829), 444.*
Review of Humboldt's works, with copious extracts.

**1830.** Slave trade.
*Eclectic Review, vol. 52 (July 1830), 22.*
Considers the slave trade upon information furnished by Humboldt's "Personal
narrative."

**1830.** Cuba. Statistical account.
*American Quarterly Review, vol. 7 (June 1830), 475.*
Review of "Cuadro estadistico," with copious extracts.

**1831.** History of Cuba.
*American Quarterly Review, vol. 10 (Sept. 1831), 230.*
Survey of the history of Cuba to 1761, drawn from Arrate's History.

**1831.** Voyages en Amérique. L'île de Cuba. Eugène Ney.
*Revue des deux Mondes, vols. 3, 4, 445.*

**1836.** Letters on Cuba, by a French gentleman.
*Blackwood, vol. 40 (Sept. 1836), 323.*

**1837.** Slavery in Cuba. F. W. P. Greenwood.
*Christian Examiner, vol. 23 (Sept. 1837), 82.*

**1840.** The currency of Cuba.
*Hunt's Merch. Mag., vol. 2 (June 1840), 531.*
Letter from a merchant in Havana, Nov. 20, 1839.

**1841.** Les esclaves dans les colonies espagnoles. Comtesse Merlin.
*Revue des deux Mondes, vol. 41 (June 1, 1841), 734.*

**1842-43.** Commerce of Cuba.
*Hunt's Merch. Mag., 7 (Oct. 1842), 319; 9 (Oct. 1843), 337.*
Statistics of imports and exports. 1839-42.

**1844.** Letters from Cuba. R. B. Kimball.
> Knickerbocker, vol. 24 (Nov. 1844), 449; (Dec. 1844), 545. Vol. 25 (Jan. 1845), 1; (Feb. 1845), 145. Vol. 26 (July–Dec. 1845), 36, 383, 544.
>> Sympathetic descriptions of the social and political condition of Cuba.

**1844.** Present state of Cuba.
> Democratic Review, vol. 15 (Nov. 1844), 475.
>> Consists of a reprint of a "Memorial on the present state of Cuba, addressed to the Spanish Government by a native of the island," with some preliminary observations.

**1845.** The Countess Merlin's letters from the Havana. J. F. Otis.
> Godey, vol. 30 (May 1845), 211.
>> On the manners and customs of Cuba.

**1845.** Le traité à Cuba et le droit de visite. X. Durrieu.
> Rev. d. d. Mondes, vol. 61 (Mar. 1, 1845), 899.
>> Review of J. A. Saco's " La supresion del tráfico de esclavos africanos en la isla de Cuba."

**1847.** L'île de Cuba et la liberté commerciale aux colonies. Félix Clavé.
> Revue des deux Mondes, vol. 18 (Juin 1847), 842.

**1847.** Cuba: and its political economy. G. L. Ditson.
> Hunt's Merch. Mag., vol. 17 (Sept. 1847), 265.

**1849.** Cuba: political conditions, etc.
> Democratic Review, vol. 25 (Sept. 1849), 193.
>> Criticises President Taylor's proclamation against filibusters, and favors acquisition of Cuba.

**1849.** Cuba: the key of the Mexican Gulf, with reference to the coast trade of the United States.
> Hunt's Merch. Mag., vol. 24 (Nov. 1849), 519.
>> Advocates acquisition of Cuba.

**1849.** Commerce and resources of Cuba.
> Hunt's Merch. Mag., vol. 21 (July 1849), 34.
>> Translated from the " Diario de la marina," Havana, Jan. 1849. Brief survey of the growth of commerce from 1828 to 1847.

**1829.** The Island of Cuba: its resources, progress, and prospects.
> Dublin Review, vol. 27 (Sept. 1849), 123.
>> Review of Madden's book on the slave trade.

**1849.** Letters from Cuba. W. C. Bryant.
> Littell's Living Age, vol. 22 (July 1849), 11.

**1849.** The poetry of Cuba. H. W. Hurlbut.
> North American Review, vol. 68 (Jan. 1849), 137.

**1859.** A trip to Cuba. J. W. Howe.
> Atlantic, vol. 3 (May, June, 1859), 601, 686; (Aug., Sept., Oct., Nov., 1859), 184, 323, 455, 602.

**1850.** The attack on Cuba (Lopez expedition).
> Littell's Living Age, vol. 26 (July 2, 1850), 141.
>> Editorials from The Examiner of London.

**1850.** Cuba et la propagande annexioniste. G. d'Alaux.
> Revue des deux Mondes, vol. 88 (July 15, 1850), 363.

**1850.** Cuba—its position, dimensions, and population. J. C. Reynolds.
> De Bow's Review, vol. 8 (April 1850), 313.

**1850.** The Island of Cuba. Its resources, progress, and prospects.
*Hogg's Instructor, N. S., vol. 4, (285).*

**1850.** The late Cuban expedition (Lopez): Military spirit of our country; its dangers, our natural duties, etc.  J. B. De Bow.
*De Bow's Review, vol. 9 (Aug. 1850), 164.*
> In favor of Cuban acquisition.

**1850.** The Cuban expedition.
*Brownson's Quarterly Review, N. S., vol. 4 (Oct. 1850), 490.*
> Review of Kimball's Cuba and the Cubans. Denounces the Lopez expedition and disapproves the policy of annexation.

**1850.** The Island of Cuba.
*Frasier's Magazine, vol. 42 (July 1850), 107; Littell's Living Age, vol. 26 (Aug. 24, 1850), 347.*
> On the political and commercial importance of Cuba in "the sight of both England and America."

**1850.** Cuba and the Cubans, Kimball's.  R. W. Griswold.
*Littell, vol. 25 (May 1850). 374.*

**1850.** General Lopez, the Cuban patriot.
*Democratic Review, vol. 26 (Feb. 1850), 97.*
> Favorable.

**1851.** The United States and Cuba.
*Dublin Univ. Mag., vol. 37 (June 1851), 763.*
> Review of J. G. Taylor's The United States and Cuba.

**1851.** Cuba and the Slave States.
*Colburn's New Monthly Magazine, vol. 93 (Oct. 1851), 218.*
> Hostile to American designs on Cuba.

**1851.** Narciso Lopez and his companions.
*Democratic Review, vol. 29 (Oct. 1851), 291.*
> Sympathetic sketch.

**1851.** La société et la littérature à Cuba.  C. de Mazade.
*Revue des deux Mondes, vol. 88 (Dec. 15, 1851), 1017.*

**1852.** The invasion of Cuba (Lopez expedition.)
*So. Q. Rev., vol. 5 (Jan. 1852), 1.*

**1852.** The Cuban debate.
*Democratic Review, vol. 31 (Nov. and Dec. 1852), 433.*
> On the debate December 23 upon the Cuban resolution. Criticises Mason and Cass.

**1852.** The late Cuban State trials.
*Democratic Review, vol. 30 (Apr. 1852), 307.*
> On the trials of filibusters at New Orleans and New York.

**1852.** Cuba, Adventures in. (Lopez expedition.)  L. Schlesinger.
*Democratic Review, vol. 31 (Sept. 1852), 210; (Oct. 1852), 352; (Nov. and Dec. 1852), 553.*
> By a participant.

**1852.** Recollections of Cuba.  W. E. Surtees.
*Colburn, vol. 94 (Feb. 1852), 208.*

**1852.** The Spaniards at Havana and the Whigs at Washington.
*Democratic Review (Oct. 1852), 326.*
> Criticises Pierce's administration.

**1853.** Cuba and the United States. The Policy of annexation discussed. W. J. Sykes.
*De Bow's Review, vol. 14 (Jan. 1853).*

**1853.** Cuba and the United States. How the interests of Louisiana would be affected by annexation. J. S. Thrasher.
*De Bow's Review, vol. 17 (July 1854), 43.*

**1853.** La Havane et l'Île de Cuba. J. J. Ampère.
*Revue des deux Mondes, vol. 95 (July 15, 1853), 305.*

**1853.** The Island of Cuba—past and present. A. W. Ely.
*De Bow's Review, vol. 14 (Feb. 1853), 93.*

**1853.** Cuba. Independence of. W. J. Sykes.
*De Bow's Review, vol. 14 (May 1853), 417.*

**1853.** Three weeks in Cuba. By an artist.
*Harper's Magazine, vol. 6 (Jan. 1853), 161.*

**1854.** Cuba and the Cubans. H. F. Bond.
*North American Review, 79 (July 1854), 109.*
>      Review of Kimball's Cuba and the Cubans; and Everett's letter to the Count de Sartiges.

**1854.** Cuba and the South.
*De Bow's Review, vol. 17 (Nov. 1854), 519.*
>      For annexation.

**1854.** Cuba and the tripartite treaty. E. B. B.
*Southern Quarterly Review, vol. 9 (Jan. 1854), 1.*
>      Review of Everett's letter to Lord John Russell, Sept. 21, 1853; Calhoun's letter to W. R. King, Aug. 12, 1844. Favors acquisition of Cuba.

**1854.** Cuba as it is in 1854. A. W. Ely.
*De Bow's Review, vol. 17 (Sept. 1854), 219.*
>      Criticism of "Compendio de geografia . . . de la Isla de Cuba." Treats of the Population—Army—Navy—Railroads—Education—Productions.

**1854.** Mr. Everett and the Cuban question. W. H. Trescott.
*Southern Quarterly Review, vol. 25, (Apr. 1854), 429.*
>      Review of Mr. Everett's letter to Lord John Russell, printed in "The correspondence on the proposed tripartite convention relative to Cuba."

**1855.** Annexation of Cuba.
*Littell, vol. 47 (Dec. 1855), 811.*
>      Brief article opposing annexation.

**1855.** Cuba. The foreign policy of the United States.
*Western Review, vol. 64 (July 1855), 181.*

**1855.** Cuba. Its present condition; the revenue, taxes, agricultural industry, etc., of the Island. A. W. Ely.
*De Bow's Review, vol. 18 (Feb. 1855), 163.*

**1855.** Reminiscences of Cuba.
*So. Lit. Mess., vol. 21 (Sept., Oct., Nov., Dec., 1855), 566, 593, 700, 745.*
>      Gives some account of the political events, the deaths of Ramón Pinto and Estrampes, etc., but mostly describes the country, people, etc.

**1855.** Spanish and Cuban views of annexation. A. W. Ely.
*De Bow's Review, vol. 18 (March 1855), 305.*

**1856.** Cuba: its state and prospects.
*London Quarterly Review, vol. 7 (Oct. 1857), 98.*

——— *Same. Eclectic Magazine, vol. 39, 406.*
> Review of Humboldt's Essai Politique; Madden's "Cuba;" Hurlbut's "Gau-Eden," and H. A. Murray's Lands of the Slave and Free.

**1859.** The acquisition of Cuba.
*Democratic Review, vol. 43 (Apr. 1859), 1.*
> Advocates annexation.

**1859.** The acquisition of Cuba. Are the United States justified in demanding the immediate surrender of Cuba?
*Hunt's Merch. Mag. vol 40 (May 1859), 562.*

**1859.** Cuban literature.
*Chambers, J., vol. 32 (Nov. 5, 1859), 290. Littell, vol. 20 (Jan. 1860), 37.*
> Principally relates to the poems of Heredia and Placido.

**1859.** On the acquisition of Cuba. F. O. J. Smith.
*Hunt's Merch. Mag., vol. 40 (Apr. 1859), 403.*

**1859.** La question de Cuba aux États-Unis et en Europe. J. Chanut.
*Revue contemporaine, vol. 43 (Apr. 1859), 470.*

**1859.** Trade and Commerce of Cuba.
*Hunt's Merch. Mag., vol. 40, 275.*

**1863.** The conquest of Cuba. C. C. Hazewell.
*Atlantic, vol. 12 (Oct., 1863), 462.*
> On the English conquest of Havana in 1762 and its restoration by the treaty of 1763; with some observations on the historical consequences.

**1865.** The Chinese in Cuba. H. B. Auchinloss.
*Hunt's Merch. Mag., vol. 52 (Mar. 1865), 186.*
> In relation to slave labor.

**1865.** Sugar making in Cuba. H. B. Auchinloss.
*Harper's Magazine, vol. 30 (Mar. 1865), 440.*

**1866.** Cuba et les Antilles. E. Duvergier de Hauranne.
*Revue des deux Mondes, Sept. 1, 15, Oct. 1, 1866.*

**1866.** Cuba, its resources and destiny.
*National Quarterly Review, vol. 14 (Dec. 1866), 35.*
> Review of Ramón de la Sagra. Historia, etc.
>> Torre J. M. de la Humboldt. Essai politique.
>> ——— compendio de geogr., etc.
>> Dana. To Cuba and back; Abbot. Letters.

**1868.** "La reina de las Antillas."
*Lippincott, vol. 1 (Apr. 1868), 423.*
> Descriptive sketch.

**1869.** Cuba sous la domination Espagnole. V. de Rochas.
*Revue Contemporaine, vol. 105 (Aug. 1869), 635.*
> The English translation was published in pamphlet form. See p. 19 of this list.

**1869.** The Cuban case. E. L. Godkin.
*Nation, vol. 9 (Sept. 30, 1869), 264.*
> Disapproves recognition of Cuban belligerency.

**1869.** L'esclavage à Cuba depuis la révolution de 1868.   A. Cochin.
*Rerue des deux Mondes, vol. 81 (May 1, 1869), 158.*

**1869.** Les Antilles espagnoles et la politique des États-Unis.
*Revue contemporaine, vol. 103 (Mar. 1869), 138.*

**1869.** L'insurrection cubaine, careses, incidens, solution possible.   A. Cochut.
*Revue des deux Mondes, vol. 188 (Nov. 15, 1869), 43.*

**1869.** The Cuban insurrection.
*The Nation, vol. 8 (April 15, 1869), 288.*
Opposes recognition of Cuban belligerency.

**1869.** Our supposed sympathy with Cuba.   A. G. Sedgwick.
*The Nation, vol. 24 (July 8, 1869), 24.*
Hostile to Cuba.

**1869.** The revolution in Cuba.   W. W. Nevin.
*Lippincott, vol. 3 (Mar. 1869), 339.*

**1870.** Cuba and Spain.
*Putnam, vol. 15 (Jan. 1870), 9.*
Urges interference by the United States.

**1870.** Coffee grounds of Cuba.
*All the Year Round, vol. 24 (June 18, 1870), 61.*

**1870.** Impressions of Cuba.   R. K.
*Monthly Rel. Mag., vol. 43 (Jan., June, 1870), 66, 562.*

**1871.** Life in Cuba.   H. S. Conant.
*Harper's Magazine, vol. 43 (Aug. 1871), 350.*

**1871.** Prison life in Cuba.
*All the Year Round, vol. 25 (Feb. 4, 1871), 222.*

**1873.** Cuba: commercial relations with the United States; geography, climate, and products.
*The Republic, vol. 1 (Aug. 1873), 325.*
Forms Cuban independence.

**1873.** The Cuban Insurrection.
*Edinburgh Review, vol. 138 (Oct. 1873), 395.*

**1873.** Cuba and the Cuban insurrection.   W. J. Starks.
*Scribner's Monthly, vol. 6 (May 1873), 10.*
Sympathetic in tone toward Cuba.

**1873.** The "Virginius."   J. N. Pomeroy; E. L. Godkin.
*The Nation, vol. 17 (Nov. 20, 1873), 333.*

**1874.** The Great Cuban difficulty.   G. A. Sala.
*Belgravia, vol. 22 (Jan. 1874), 311.*

**1874.** La question cubaine.   Six ans d'insurrection.
*Rev. d. d. Mondes, vol. 214 (Mar. 15, 1874), 434.*

**1875.** Free glances at Cuba.   G. A. F. Van Rhyn.
*Appleton's Journal, vol. 13 (Mar. 1875), 353.*
Sketches of life in Cuba.

**1875.** The Cuban scare and the press.   A. G. Sedgwick.
   *The Nation, vol. 21 (Nov. 1875), 335.*

**1876.** The state of Cuba.   R. B. Mintarn.
   *The Nation, vol. 22 (Feb. 17, 1876), 110.*

**1879.** Our commerce with Cuba, Porto Rico, and Mexico.   C. C. Andrews.
   *Atlantic, rol. 44 (July 1879), 81.*

**1881.** The currency and commerce of Cuba.   D. P. Bailey.
   *Banker's Magazine, vol. 35 (Mar. 1881), 697.*

**1881.** Impressions of Havana and Cuba.   W. H. Bishop.
   *The Nation, rol. 32 (May 5, 1881), 312.*
       On the lottery, mode of life, political jobbery, etc.

**1892.** La exploitacion de una colonia.   Ensayo histórico, crítico sobre los subsidios
   de Cuba á la nación.   Mannuel Villanova.
   *Revista Cubana, Tomo 16 (Sept. 1892), 157.*

**1892.** Spain and the United States.   R. Ogden.
   *Chautauquan, vol. 14, p. 565.*

**1893.** Mr. Marcy, the Cuban Question, and the Ostend Manifesto.   S. Webster.
   *Political Science Quarterly, rol. 8 (Mar. 1893), 1.*

**1893.** Business Opportunities in Cuba.   E. J. Chibas.
   *Engineering Mag., vol. 4, p. 266.*

**1894.** Filibustering Expeditions to Cuba in 1860.   R. F. Logan.
   *Southern Magazine, vol. 4, p. 608.*

**1894.** Tertiary and later history of Cuba.   R. T. Hill.
   *American Journal of Science, rol. 148, p. 196.*

**1894.** Women of Cuba.   M. E. Springer.
   *North American Review, vol. 158 (Feb. 1894), 255.*

**1895.** The Spanish colonies.
   *Spectator, rol. 74 (Apr. 6, 1895), 453.*

**1895.** Symposium.
   *Independent, Dec. 5, 1895.*

**1895.** Struggle for Freedom.   J. F. Clark.
   *Cosmopolitan, vol. 19, p. 608.*

**1895.** Struggle for Freedom.   M. García.
   *Mo. Illus. May, vol. 11 (Oct. 1895), 227.*

**1895.** Spain and Cuba.   R. Ogden.
   *Nation, vol. 60 (Apr. 25, 1895), 319.*

**1895.** A Glimpse of Cuba.   J. K. Reeve.
   *Lippincott, vol. 55 (Mar. 1895), 319.*

**1895.** Cuba—How it might have belonged to France.   G. Colmache.
   *Littell's Living Age, vol. 207, p. 696.*

**1895.** Ought we to annex Cuba?   F. R. Coudert and others.
   *American Mag. of Civics, vol. 7, p. 37.*

**1895.** Problem of Cuba.
   *Spectator, rol. 75 (Sept. 21, 1895), 357.*

**1895.** Revolt in Cuba—its causes and effects. A native Cuban.
*Engineering Mag., vol. 10, p. 9.*

**1895.** Shall Cuba be free? Clarence King.
*Forum, vol. 20 (Sept. 1895), 50.*

**1895.** Situation in Cuba. S. Alvarez.
*Mo. Am., vol. 161, p. 362.*

**1895.** Cuba's Struggle for Freedom. J. F. Clark.
*Cosmopolitan, vol. 19 (Oct. 1875), 608.*

**1895.** Sympathy for Cuba. R. Ogden.
*Nation, rol. 61, p. 250.*

**1896.** Commercial relations between Cuba and the United States. E. S. Gould.
*Engineering Mag., vol. 7, p. 500.*

**1896.** Cuba, our neighbor in the sea. F. H. Osborne.
*Chautauquan, vol. 23 (May 1896), 202.*

**1896.** Our Cuban neighbors and their struggle for liberty. M. Halstead.
*Review of Reviews, vol. 13 (Apr. 1896), 419.*

**1896.** Claims of Cuba for self-government. R. Cabrera.
*Gunton's Magazine, vol. 11, p. 423.*

**1896.** Fire and sword in Cuba. Clarence King.
*Forum, vol. 22 (Sept. 1896), 31.*

**1896.** Five Weeks with the Insurgents. H. Howard.
*Contemporary Review, vol. 69 (Jan. 1896), 41*

**1896.** Industrial Cuba. E. Vasquez.
*Gunton's Magazine, vol. 10, p. 447.*

**1896.** Industrial possibilities of Cuba. R. Cabrera.
*Engin. Mag., vol. 11, p. 875.*

**1896.** Negroes in Cuba and the Revolution.
*Gunton's Magazine, vol. 11, p. 272.*

**1896.** Cuba and the United States.
*National Magazine, vol. 27, p. 449.*

**1896.** The question of Cuban belligerency. J. B. Moore.
*Forum, vol. 21 (May 1896), 288.*

**1896.** Recognition of belligerency of Cuba. A. S. Hershey.
*Am. Acad. Pol. Sci., vol. 7, p. 450.*

**1896.** Grant's Precedent on Recognition of Cuba.
*The Nation, vol. 62 (Feb. 13, 1896), 137.*

**1896.** A Cuban Catechism. A. C. Sedgwick.
*Nation, vol. 62 (Mar. 12, 1896), 211.*

**1896.** Causes of Present War in Cuba. H. L. De Zayes.
*Catholic World, vol. 62 (Mar. 1896), 807.*

**1896.** Our duty to Cuba. H. C. Lodge.
*Forum, vol. 21 (May 1896), 278.*

**1896.** Question of Cuba. J. Maurice Kelley.
*New Review, vol. 15, p. 144*

**1896.** Possible Complications of Cuba.  M. W. Hazeltine.
*North American Review, vol. 162 (April 1896), 406.*

**1896.** Revolt in Cuba.  W. S. Churchill.
*Saturday Review, vol. 81 (Feb. 15, 1896), 165 ; vol. 82 (Aug. 29, 1896), 213.*

**1896.** War in Cuba and the Spanish Treasury.
*Gunton's Magazine, vol. 11 (Aug. 1896), 122.*

**1896.** What shall be done about Cuba?  M. W. Hazeltine.
*North American Review, vol. 163 (Dec. 1896), 731.*

**1897.** The United States and Cuba.  W. Hallett-Phillips.
*National Review, Jan. 1897.*

**1897.** The present and future of Cuba.  F. G. Pierra.
*Forum, vol. 22 (Feb. 1897), 659.*

**1897.** Spain and Cuba.  James H. Babcock.
*Chautauquan, vol. 24 (Feb. 1897), 584.*

**1897.** Analysis of Cuban Population.  Raimundo Cabrera.
*Gunton's Magazine, Mar. 1897.*

**1897.** The United States and Cuba.  Henry Rochefort.
*Forum, Apr. 1897.*

**1897.** Why Spain has failed in Cuba.  T. G. Alvord, Jr.
*Forum, vol. 23 (July 1897), 564.*

**1897.** The Cuban Revolt.
*Current History, vol. 7 (June 30, 1897), 338.*

**1897.** Cuba, Spain, and the United States.  C. Benoist.
*Chautauquan, vol. 25 (July 1897), 384.*

**1897.** Cuba and Spain.  B. J. Clinch.
*Amer. Catholic Quarterly Rev., Nov. 1897.*

**1897.** Review of Reviews, vol. 15.
        Death of Maceo, p. 10.
        Mr. Cleveland on the Rebellion, p. 10.
        Canovas to America, p. 11.
        Cameron Resolution, p. 11.
        Cuban Outlook, pp. 12, 258.
        Cuban Question at Washington, pp. 69, 134, 402.
        Cuban Question in Cuba, p. 136.
        American Friends of Cuba, p. 137.
        The United States and Cuba, pp. 197–591.
        Spain's Reform Plan for Cuba, p. 259.
        Cuban Revolutionary Government, p. 329.
        Real Condition of Cuba to-day, p. 562.
        Steps toward Relief of Cuba, p. 643.
        Crete and Cuba compared, p. 644.
        Demand for Intervention, p. 644.
        Sugar affecting Cuba's Fate, p. 645.

**1897.** The Cuban Question.  Hannis Taylor.
*North American Review, vol. 165 (Nov. 1897), 610.*

**1897.** The situation in Spain.  S. Bonsal.
*Review of Reviews, vol. 16 (Nov. 1897), 555.*

**1897.** Insurrection in Cuba and American neutrality.
*Amer. Law Rev., vol. 31 (Jan., Feb.), 62.*

**1897.** Provisional Government of Cuba.   F. W. Steep.
*Arena, vol. 17 (Aug. 1897).*

**1897.** Is the Cuban capable of self-government?   T. G. Alvord, Jr.
*Forum, vol. 24 (Sept. 1897), 119.*

**1897.** Liberation of Spanish-American colonies.   H. D. Money.
*North American Review, vol. 165 (Sept. 1897), 256.*

**1897.** American annexation and armament.   Murat Halstead.
*Forum, vol. 24 (Sept. 1897), 56.*

**1898.** The Spanish Crisis.
*Blackwood's Magazine, vol. 163 (Feb. 1898), 238.*

**1898.** The starving Cubans.   S. Scovel.
*Presbyterian Banner, Feb. 23, 1898, 3.*

**1898.** The situation in Cuba to-day.   E. B. Hastings.
*National Magazine, vol. 7 (Mar. 1898), 552.*

**1898.** Intervention of the United States in Cuba.   J. H. Latané.
*North American Review, vol. 166 (Mar. 1898), 350.*

**1898.** Cuban autonomy or independence?
*The Nation, vol. 66 (Mar. 10, 1898), 178.*

# GOVERNMENT DOCUMENTS.

### (EXCLUSIVE OF RESOLUTIONS, BILLS AND SPEECHES).

---

**1822.** Cuba. Decree (Spain). Foreign trade. Jan. 27, Feb. 4, 1822.
*British and foreign state papers, vol. 10, p. 865.*

**1822-53.** Cuba. Correspondence. Great Britain and France, etc. Alleged projects of conquest and annexation.
*British and foreign state papers, vol. 44, p. 114.*

**1822-1837.** Cuba. Correspondence. Spain and the United States.
*British and foreign state papers, vol. 26, p. 1124.*

**1823.** Cuba. Decree (Spain). Exclusion of vessels and goods of Austria, France, Prussia, and Russia.
*British and foreign state papers, vol. 10, p. 1034.*

**1823.** Cuba. Decree (Spain). Foreign trade. Liquidation of British Claims.
*British and foreign state papers, vol. 10, p. 867, 1034.*

**1825-6.** Cuba. Correspondence. Colombia and the United States.
*British and foreign state papers, vol. 13, p. 126, 414.*

**1825-6.** Cuba. Correspondence. Mexico and the United States.
*British and foreign state papers, vol. 13, p. 426.*

**1825-6.** Cuba. Correspondence. France and the United States.
*British and foreign state papers, vol. 13, p. 424, 443.*

**1825-6.** Cuba. Correspondence. Russia and the United States.
*British and foreign state papers, vol. 13, p. 403, 490.*

**1828.** Cuba. Royal order (Spain). Disposal of emancipated slaves. Apr. 15, 1828.
*British and foreign state papers, vol. 20, p. 1289.*

**1834.** Trade between United States and Cuba and Porto Rico. Message of the President, March 8, 1834. 44 pp.
*Twenty-third Cong., first sess., Ex. Doc. No. 170.*

**1834.** Tonnage duties. Cuba and Porto Rico. May 17, 1834.
*Twenty-third Cong., first sess., House Report No. 468.*

**1835.** Commerce with Cuba and Porto Rico. Message from the President in relation to the commerce of the United States with the Spanish ports of Cuba and Porto Rico. February 3, 1835. 7 pp.
*Twenty-third Cong., first sess., Ex. Doc. No. 120.*

**1837.** Cuba. Correspondence. Great Britain and the United States. American policy.
*British and foreign state papers, vol. 26, p. 1156.*

S. Doc. 161——3                                                        33

**1838.** Cuba. Circular of Governor-General. Prohibition against landing of free blacks. June 12, 1838.
*British and foreign state papers, vol. 27, p. 363.*

**1838.** Cuba. Royal order (Spain.) Nonintroduction of black slaves. Nov. 2, 1838.
*British and foreign state papers, vol. 27, p. 379.*

**1840-44.** Cuba. Correspondence. Spain and United States. American policy.
*British and foreign state papers, vol. 32, p. 861.*

**1845.** Cuba. Correspondence. Great Britain and Spain. Admission of sugars into Great Britain upon same terms as sugars of United States and Venezuela. May–Dec. 1845.
*British and foreign state papers, vol. 33, p. 949.*

**1849.** Cuba. Proclamation. United States. Threatened invasion. Aug. 11, 1844.
*British and foreign state papers, vol. 39, p. 77.*

**1849.** Message from the President to both Houses of Congress, December 24, 1849.
*Thirty-first Cong., first sess., Ex. Doc. No. 5*
     Page 27 contains Proclamation against filibustering expedition.

**1850.** Message from the President, transmitting reports from the several heads of departments relative to the subject of alleged revolutionary movements in Cuba, June 3, 1850. 134 pp.
*Thirty-first Cong., first sess., Senate Doc. No. 57.*

**1851.** Cuba. Proclamation. United States prohibition against fitting out of an expedition for invasion of Cuba. Apr. 25, 1851.
*British and foreign state papers, vol. 47, p. 1265.*

**1851.** Message from the President to both Houses of Congress, December 2, 1851.
*Thirty-second Cong., first sess., Senate Doc. No. 1; Ex. Doc. No. 2.*
     Page 27 contains Proclamation against filibustering expeditions.

**1851.** Message from the President, communicating the correspondence relative to any projected expedition to the island of Cuba, not heretofore communicated, February 27, 1851. 90 pp.
*Thirty-first Cong., second sess., Senate Doc. No. 41.*

**1851** John S. Thrasher. Message from the President, communicating information in regard to the imprisonment of J. S. Thrasher at Havana.
*Thirty-second Cong., first sess., Senate Doc. No. 5; Ex. Doc. No. 10.*

**1852.** Cuba. Correspondence. Spain and United States. Policy of United States.
*British and foreign state papers, vol. 44, p. 133.*

**1852.** John S. Thrasher. Message from the President, transmitting further information respecting the imprisonment, etc., of John S. Thrasher, January 2, 1852. 87 pp.
*Thirty-second Cong., first sess., Ex. Doc. No. 14.*

**1852.** Lopez expedition. Message from the President, transmitting a report in reference to the Lopez expedition, January 5, 1852.
*Thirty-second Cong., first sess., Ex. Doc. No. 19.*

**1852.** Barque Georgiana and brig Susan Loud. Message from the President, transmitting information in reference to the seizure and confiscation. March 23, 1852.
*Thirty-second Cong., first sess., Ex. Doc. No. 83.*

**1852.** Foreigners. Cuban expedition. Message from the President of the United States, transmitting a report in reference to such of the Cuban prisoners as were foreigners. July 7, 1852. 87 pp.

*Thirty-second Cong., first sess., Ex. Doc. No. 115.*

**1852.** Island of Cuba. Message from the President of the United States in reference to the Island of Cuba, July 13, 1852.

*Thirty-second Cong., first sess., Ex. Doc. No. 121. 59 pp. 8°.*

Transmitting instructions to diplomatic agents relating to the policy of the Government of the United States in relation to Cuba, from 1822 to 1848.

**1853.** Cuba. Correspondence. Great Britain and United States. Proposed tripartite convention between Great Britain, France, and United States.

*British and foreign state papers, vol. 44, p. 231.*

**1853.** Message from the President relative to a proposed tripartite convention on the subject of Cuba, January 4, 1853. 23 pp.

*Thirty-second Cong., second sess., Senate Doc. No. 13.*

This document was reprinted, together with Everett's Letter to Lord John Russell, under the title "Correspondence on the proposed tripartite convention," by Little, Brown & Co., of Boston. (*See* p. 10, of this List.)

**1854.** Message from the President of the United States, transmitting a copy of the correspondence in relation to the imprisonment of James H. West in the Island of Cuba. March 11, 1854. 54 pp.

*Thirty-third Cong., first sess., Senate Doc. No. 46.*

**1854.** Seizure of the Black Warrior. Message of the President of the United States, transmitting a report in reference to the seizure of the Black Warrior. March 15, 1854. 34 pp.

*Thirty-third Cong., first sess., Ex. Doc. No. 76.*

**1854.** Case of the Black Warrior, and other violations of the rights of American citizens by Spanish authorities. Message of the President of the United States, April 6, 1854. 378 pp.

*Thirty-third Cong., first sess., Ex. Doc. No. 86.*

**1854.** Cuba. Proclamation. United States. Prohibition against fitting out of an expedition for invasion of Cuba. May 31, 1854.

*British and foreign state papers, vol. 47, p. 1266.*

**1855.** The Ostend conference, etc. Message from the President, transmitting correspondence touching matters disturbing the friendly relations between this Government and the Government of Spain; also a report as to the objects of the meeting of the American ministers at Ostend, March 3, 1855. 152 pp.

*Thirty-third Cong., second sess., House Ex. Doc. No. 93.*

**1859.** In the Senate of the United States. Report of the Committee on Foreign Relations, to whom was referred the bill "making appropriations to facilitate the acquisition of the Island of Cuba by negotiations." 26 pp.

*Thirty-fifth Cong., second sess., Senate Report No. 351.*

**1859.** Report of the Secretary of the Treasury, in answer to a resolution of the Senate, calling for statistics of trade with Cuba for the last five years. March 2, 1859. 19 pp.

*Thirty-fifth Cong., second sess., Senate Doc. No. 45.*

**1860.** Cuba. Decree (Spain). Introduction of Chinese laborers into Island of Cuba.

*British and foreign state papers, vol. 51, p. 1038.*

**1860.** Imprisonment of an American citizen in the Island of Cuba. Message from the President of the United States, March 30, 1860. 8 pp.
*Thirty-sixth Cong., first sess., Ex. Doc. No. 54.*

**1865.** Cuba. Decree (Spain). Extinction of slavery in Cuba.
*British and foreign state papers, vol. 56, p. 1327.*

**1869.** Message of the President of the United States communicating, in compliance with a resolution of the Senate, information in regard to the progress of the revolution in Cuba, and the political and civil condition of the island. 118 pp.
*Forty-first Cong., second sess., Senate Ex. Doc. No. 7.*

**1870.** Struggle for independence in the Island of Cuba. Message of the President of the United States, transmitting correspondence relative to the struggle for freedom in the Island of Cuba, February 21, 1870. 193 pp.
*Forty-first Cong., second sess., House Ex. Doc. No. 160.*

**1870.** Message from the President, communicating information and making certain recommendations in relation to the existing insurrection in Cuba.
*Forty-first Cong., second sess., Senate Doc. No. 99.*

**1870.** Message from the President communicating information in relation to the seizure of American vessels, and injuries to American citizens in Cuba, July 9, 1870.
*Forty-first Cong., second sess., Senate Doc. No. 108.*

**1870.** Message of the President of the United States communicating, in compliance with the resolution of the Senate of the 8th instant, information in relation to the emancipation of slaves in Cuba, July 14, 1870. 24 pp.
*Forty-first Cong., second sess., Senate Ex. Doc. No. 113.*

**1871.** Agreement for settlement of certain claims of citizens of the United States on account of wrongs and injuries committed by authorities of Spain in the Island of Cuba. Concluded at Madrid, February 11-12, 1871.
*[In Treaties and Conventions from 1776-1887. Washington (1889). pp. 1025-1027.]*

**1872.** Cuba. Spanish regulation. Abolition of slavery.
*British and foreign state papers, vol. 63, p. 437.*

**1872.** Message from the President, relative to questions with Spain growing out of affairs with Cuba.
*Forty-second Cong., second sess., Senate Doc. No. 32.*

**1872.** Reindenture or reenslavement of Chinamen in Cuba. Message from the President, March 20, 1872. 15 pp.
*Forty-second Cong., second sess., Ex. Doc. No. 207.*

**1874.** Cuba. Circular (Spain). Port dues.
*British and foreign state papers, vol. 66, p. 1178.*

**1876.** Cuba. Decree. Emancipados.
*British and foreign state papers, vol. 67, p. 406.*

**1876.** Correspondence between the United States Government and Spain in relation to the Island of Cuba. Message from the President, transmitting a report from the Secretary of State, with accompanying documents, January 31, 1876. 81 pp.
*Forty-fourth Cong., first sess., House Ex. Doc. No. 90.*

**1877.** Cuba. Convention. China and Spain. Emigration.
*British and foreign state papers, vol. 69, p. 364.*

**1878.** Message from the President communicating information respecting the terms
and conditions under which the surrender of the Cuban insurgents has
been made, and in relation to the future policy of Spain in the government of the island of Cuba, May 14, 1878. 23 pp.
*Forty-fifth Cong., second sess., Senate Doc., No. 79.*

**1881.** Cuba. Decree (Spain). Promulgation in Cuba of constitution of monarchy.
Apr. 7, 1881.
*British and foreign state papers, vol. 73, p. 269.*

**1884.** Cuba. Agreement. United States and Spain. Commercial relations. Jan.
2, 1884.
*British and foreign state papers, vol. 75, pp. 389, 390.*

**1886.** Cuba. Decree (Spain). Abolition. Patronage system. Emancipated slaves.
*British and foreign state papers, vol. 77, p. 825.*

**1887.** Cuba. Proclamation (U. S.). Discriminating duties. Vessels from Cuba,
Sept. 21, 1887.
*British and foreign state papers, vol. 78, p. 43.*

**1887.** Cuba. Agreement. United States and Spain. Abolition. Discriminating
duties. September 21, 1887.
*British and foreign state papers, vol. 78, p. 44.*

**1892.** Statement of exports to Cuba since reciprocity treaty.
*Fifty-second Cong., first sess., Ex. Doc. No. 107.*

**1893.** Sugar in Cuba. Report of Commercial Agent Mullen. 1893.
*In U. S. Consular Report No. 152. p. 255.*

**1894.** Cuban sugar exports.
*U. S. Consular Report No. 171. p. 567.*

**1894.** Sugar exports from Cuba.
*U. S. Consular Report No. 170. p. 393.*

**1894.** Tobacco interests of Cuba.
*U. S. Consular Report No. 167. pp. 630–632.*

**1894.** Export of Cuban sugar.
*U. S. Consular Report No. 165. p. 255.*

**1894.** Iron ore and manganese in Cuba.
*U. S. Consular Report No. 161. pp. 346–7.*

**1894.** Cuba's market for American flour.
*U. S. Consular Report No. 164. p. 151.*

**1894.** Economic condition of Cuba.
*U. S. Consular Report No. 167. pp. 632–3.*

**1894.** Cuba and the eucalyptus tree.
*U. S. Consular Report No. 168. p. 20.*

**1894.** Sugar interests of Cuba.
*U. S. Consular Report No. 169. pp. 243–252.*

**1894.** Cuba's exports declared for the United States.
*U. S. Consular Report No. 171. pp. 456–7.*

**1895.** American flour in Cuba.
　　*U. S. Consular Report No. 175.　pp. 556–562.*

**1895.** Condition of Cuban sugar industry.
　　*U. S. Consular Report No. 175.　pp. 552–3.*

**1895.** Exports declared for United States by Cuba.
　　*U. S. Consular Report No. 175.　pp. 503–4.*

**1895.** Finances of Cuba.
　　*U. S. Consular Report No. 175.　pp. 554–6.*

**1895.** New tariff for Cuba.
　　*U. S. Consular Report No. 175.　pp. 562–3.*

**1895.** New tax law for Cuba.
　　*U. S. Consular Report No. 175.　p. 563.*

**1895.** Cuban sugar statistics.
　　*U. S. Consular Report No. 176.　p. 187.*

**1895.** Cuba's asphalt deposits near Cardenas.
　　*U. S. Consular Report No. 172.　pp. 126–128.*

**1895.** The sugar industry in Cuba.
　　*U. S. Consular Report No. 172.　p. 111.*

**1896.** Recognition of Cuban independence. Report (from the Committee on Foreign Relations). December 21, 1896. 103 pp.
　　*Fifty-fourth Cong., second sess., Senate Report No. 1160.*

**1896.** Power to recognize the independence of a new foreign state. Memorandum (from the Committee on Foreign Relations). December 21. 1896. 57 pp.
　　*Fifty-fourth Cong., second sess., Senate Doc. No. 56.*

The Smithsonian Institution receives the publications of the following learned societies of Cuba:

## HAVANA.

Academia de ciencias médicas, físicas, y naturales de la Habana.

Academia elemental de ciencias y letras de la Habana.

Acclimatation Station.

Administracion General de Comunicacion de la Isla de Cuba.

Administracion General de Correos de la Isla de Cuba.　(Post-office Department.)

"Archivos de la Policlínica."

Bar Association.

Biblioteca Pública.

Botanical Garden.

La Cartéra Cubana.

"Crónica Médico-quirúrgia de la Habana."

Escuela Medico-Dental.

Escuela de Sordo Mudos y Ciegos.

Facultad de Medicina.

"Havana Weekly Report." (Inspeccion General de Telégrafos. [*See* Administracion General de Comunicaciones de la Isla de Cuba.])

Instituto de Segunda Enseñanza de la Habana.

Librería Especial Pedagogia.

Marine Meteorological Service.

"Minerva."
"Miscelánico (El)."
Museo de Historia Natural.
Observatorio Físico-Meteorólogico de la Habana.
Observatorio Naval.
Observatorio del Real Colegio de Belen.
"Progreso Médico (El)."
Real Sociedad Económica de la Habana.
Real Universidad de la Habana.
"Revista de Ciencias Médicas."
"Revista de Foro."
"Revista General de Comunicaciones."
Revista Habanera.
Sociedad Antropológica de la Isla de Cuba.
Sociedad Medico-quirurgia de la Habana.

### SANTA CLARA.

Estacion Agronómica.

### SANTIAGO DE CUBA.

"Cuba Masónica."

# M. A P S

OF

# CUBA, PORTO RICO, AND THE WEST INDIES

IN THE

# LIBRARY OF CONGRESS.

(EXTRACTED FROM "MAPS OF AMERICA, A BIBLIOGRAPHY OF AMERICAN
CARTOGRAPHY," IN THE LIBRARY OF CONGRESS.)

BY

## P. LEE PHILLIPS.

# MAPS OF CUBA, PORTO RICO, AND THE WEST INDIES.

## CUBA.

**1492-1592.** Dibujo atribuido á Cristóbal Colon, que se halla unido á la traduccion latina de Cozco de la carta que aquel escribió al tesorero Sanchez. Figura de la isla de Cuba en el Isolaris de Benedeto Bordoni de 1528. Figura de la misma isla en una carta unida á una edicion de Tolomeo de 1513. Otra figura de dicha isla en una carta de Teodoro de Bry de 1592. Otra figura en una gran carta portugesa, pintada sobre pergamino, que se halla en la biblioteca real de Paris. Otra figura en la carta de Paolo Forlano, titulada La descriptione de tuto il Perú, por los años 1564 y 1565.

> [*In Sagra (Ramón de la). Historia física, política y natural de la isla de Cuba. fol. Paris, A. Bertrand, 1842. v. 2, pl. 2, fig. 1a–6a.*]

**1493-1500.** Parte correspondiente á la América de la carta general de Juan de La Cosa, piloto en el segundo viage de Cristóbal Colon en 1493, y en la expedicion de Alonzo de Hojeda en 1499. Calcada sobre la original que posee el Sr. baron de Walckenaer. Paris, 1837. 23x34.

> [*In Sagra (Ramón de la). Historia física, política y natural de la isla de Cuba. fol. Paris, A. Bertrand, 1842. v. 2.*]

**1555.** Parte de una carta del atlas universal manuscrito de Guillermo Lo Testu. 1555. 12x9.

> [*In Sagra (Ramón de la). Historia física, política y natural de la isla de Cuba. fol. Paris, A. Bertrand, 1842. v. 2, pl. 3.*]

**1564-1565.** Mapa de la isla de una coleccion de Fernando Berteli, hecha por los años de 1564 y 1565. 10x7.

> [*In Sagra (Ramón de la). Historia física, política y natural de la isla de Cuba. fol. Paris, A. Bertrand, 1842. v. 2, pl. 4.*]

**1564-1594.** Plano de la isla de Cuba de Paolo Forlano de 564. Isla de Cuba de una carta de Teodoro Bry de 1594. La misma isla de la gran carta manuscrita y pintada de Matheum Nerenum Pecciolem do 1604.

> [*In Sagra (Ramón de la). Historia física, política y natural de la isla de Cuba. fol. Paris, A. Bertrand, 1842. v. 2, pl. 5, fig. 1a–3a.*]

**1605.** Cvba insvla et Iamaica. 9x11.

> [*In Wytfliet (Cornelius) and others. Histoire vniversalle des Indies. fol. Douay, F. Fabri, 1597. facing p. 101.*]

**1607-1670.** Porcion de la costa de la isla de Cuba, gravada á principios del siglo xviii. Isla de Cuba del atlas de Hondius de 1607. Plano manuscrito de la ciudad de la Habana del depósito de la marina en Paris. Plano manuscrito conservado en mismo depósito, y que lleva por leyenda: La Havane en 1670, envoyé par m. le c. d'Estrées, snivant sa lettre do 10 octobre 1676 à Brest.

> [*In Sagra (Ramón de la). Historia física, política y natural de la isla de Cuba. fol. Paris, A. Bertrand, 1842. v. 7, fig. 1-2.*]

43

**1680.** A chart of the island of Cuba. The gulf of Florida, with the Bahama islands, and ye Windward passage. [Anon. 17x21. London, ab. 1680.]
[*American maps. v. 4, no. 35.*]
> Note.—Attributed to John Thornton.

**1695–97.** Isola Cuba. 8½x11½.
[*In Coronelli (Vincenzo). Atlante Veneto. fol. Venetia, 1695–97. v. 2, pt. 2, pp. 164–165.*]

**1752.** A new & accurate map of the island of Cuba [and] a new & accurate map of the islands of Hispaniola or St. Domingo and Porto Rico. By Eman. Bowen. 13½x16½.
[*In his A complete atlas. fol. London, for W. Innys (etc.) 1752. no. 65.*]

**1762.** A new chart of the seas, surrounding the island of Cuba, with the soundings, currents, ships' courses, etc., and a map of the island itself, lately made by an officer in the navy. (anon.) 10½x14.
[*London*] *for the London magazine, 1762.*

**1762.** An accurate map of Cuba, and the adjacent islands. Engraved A. B. (A. Bell). (Also) A plan of the city and harbour of Havana. 7x16.
[*In Scots (The) magazine. 1762. 8°. Edinburgh, W. Sands (etc. 1762). v. 24, p. 476.*]

**1763.** Carta esatta rappresentante l'isola di Cuba estratta dalle carte del sig. G. M. Terreni sc. 10x12½.
[*In Gazzettiere (Il) americano. 4°. Liroruo, M. Coltellini, 1763. v. 1, p. 140.*]

**1768.** A map of the isle of Cuba, with the Bahama islands, gulf of Florida, and Windward passage. Drawn from english and spanish surveys. (anon.) 13x19.
[*In Jefferys (T. engraver). A general topography of North America and the West Indies. fol. London, for R. Sayer & T. Jefferys, 1768. no. 79.*]

**1775.** The island of Cuba with part of the Bahama banks & the Martyrs. By Thos. Jefferys. 18½x24½. London, for R. Sayer, 1775.
[*In his The West India atlas. fol. London, for R. Sayer & J. Bennett, 1775. no. 7.*]

**1778.** Carta esatta rappresentante l' isola di Cuba. 10x12.
[*In Atlante dell' America. (anon.) fol. Liroruo, 1778. no. 13.*]

**1818.** Laurie and Whittle's new chart of the Windward passages and Bahama islands, with the islands of St. Domingo, Jamaica, Cuba, etc., etc. Compiled from a great variety of topographic surveys and nautical details. By John Purdy. 3d ed., improved 1818. London, Laurie & Whittle, sept. 2, 1811 (1818).
[*In Whittle (J.) and Laurie (R. H.) The West India atlas. fol. London, J. Whittle & R. H. Laurie. 1818, no. 11–12.*]

**1822.** Geographical, statistical, and historical map of Cuba and the Bahama islands. B. Tanner sc. 9½x14.
[*In Complete (A) historical, chronological and geographical american atlas. fol. Philadelphia, H. C. Carey & I. Lea, 1822. no. 40.*]

**1824–31.** Carta geogr°.-topográfica de la Isla de C. [Compiled by] el teniente general Conde de C. y la Comision de gefes y oficiales militares y de agrimensores públicos . . . en los años de 1824 a 1831.
(*Plano de . . . Habana, etc.*) *6 Sheets. Barcelona, 1835.*
> Note.—In Department of State.

**1826.** Carte de l'isle de Cuba. Rédigée sur les observations astronomiques des navigateurs espagnoles et sur celles de mr. de Humboldt. Par P. L. Lapie. 1826. 12½x24½.

[In Humboldt (F. H. A.) and Bonpland (A) Atlas géouraphique et physique des regions equinoxiales du nouveau continent. fol. Paris, Gide, 1814-34. pl. 23.]

**1826.** Île de Cuba. Écrit par Hacq. 9x13.

[In Huber (E.) Aperçu statistique de l'ile de Cuba. 8°. Paris, P. Dufart, 1826.]

**1831-37.** Plano comparativo de la configuracion de las costas de la extremidad occidental de la isla de Cuba, representadas en la gran carta de Barcelona de 1831 y en la del depósito hydrográfico de Madrid de 1837. 9x17.

[In Sagra (Ramón de la). Historia física, política y natural de la isla de Cuba. fol. Paris, A. Bertrand, 1842. pl. 91.]

**1841.** Plano geográfico de la isla de Cuba. 21x36.

[In Sagra (Ramón de la). Historia física, política y natural de la isla de Cuba. fol. Paris, A. Bertrand, 1842. vol. 2.]

**1850.** Wilson's statistical map of Cuba. 1850. 12x17½. New Orleans, Thomas William Wilson, (1850).

**1851.** New map of the island of Cuba showing the present theater of war. 15x20. New York, T. Schedler, 1851.

**1851.** Posesiones de America. Isla de Puerto Rico. Por el teniente coronel capitan de ingenieros d.Francisco Coello. Las notas estadísticas é históricas han sido escritas. Por d. Pascual Madoz. 33x44. Madrid, J. Noguerra, 1851.

NOTE.—At top of sheet "Diccionario—geográfico—estatistico histórico. Atlas de España—sus posesiones de ultramar." Copy in Department of State.

**1851.** Cuba. 18x23. Philadelphia, R. L. Barnes, 1851.

NOTE.—In Department of State.

**1851-53.** Isla de Cuba. Atlas del diccionario geográfico. Por F. Coello y P. Madoz 2 sheets each 33x44. Madrid, 1851-53.

NOTE.—In Department of State.

**1852-53.** Chart of the island of Cuba. John Arrowsmith, litho. 11½x24.

[In Great Britain. Parliament. Reports, committees. 1852-53. v. 39.]

**1855.** Ensign, Bridgman & Fanning. Map of the island of Cuba. Compiled from the most reliable spanish authorities. col. fold. 26x34. [New York, Ensign, Bridgman & Fanning, 1855.]

**1855.** Map of the island of Cuba. Compiled from the most reliable spanish authorities. 1855. (anon.) 25x33½. [New York, 1855.]

**1861.** Mapa físico político e itinerario de la isla de Cuba. Acompañalo de varios planos particulares y de noticias estadísticas, por d. José Maria de la Torre. 49x67. Nuevo York, J. H. Colton, 1861.

**1864.** Nuevo mapa topográfico de la isla de Puerto Rico. Con planos extensos de los principales puertos y notas estadísticas compiladas de datas oficiales. 40x58. Nueva York, J. H. Colton, 1864.

NOTE.—Contains Mapa de las Antillas y contornos de Ponce. Mapa de los contornos de S. Juan de Puerto Rico. Mapa de las yslas de Cuba y San Domingo y Jamaica. Plano de S. Juan de Puerto Roco. Mapa de la isla Culebra y Vieques y canales entre ellas y Puerto Rico, etc.
NOTE.—Copy in Department of State.

**1872.** Mapa de la isla de Cuba en 1872. Arreglado á la última division territorial [etc.] Por d. Enrique de Arantave. 12x18. fold. sq. 16°. Madrid, J. M. Penulas, grabo. 1872.

**1873.** Cuba. Western portion. Republished from Brit. admy. chart no. 2579, corrected to nov., 1873. 24½x37. Washington, 1873.
   [*United States. Navy Department. Hydrographic office, Chart no. 516.*]

**1874.** Schedler (J.) Topographical map of the island of Cuba. 22x33. 4°. New York, E. Steiger, 1874.

**1875.** Carta geo-topografica de la isla de Cuba. Por D. Estéban Pichardo. 34 of the 36 sheets. each 21x23. [Habana, 1875.]
   Note.—Sheets 33-34 wanting. i.e., title page and Puerto Rico.

**1878.** Cuba. Eastern portion. Republished from Brit. admy. chart no. 2580, corrected to jan., 1878. 28½x37. Washington, 1878.
   [*United States. Navy Department. Hydrographic office, Chart no. 517.*]

**1881.** Gran carta geográfica-enciclopédica de la isla de Cuba. Compilado por d. German Gonzales. Grabada por G. Pfeifer. Lit. de G. Pfeifer. Madrid 33x62.
   *Habana, publicada por la propaganda literaria, 1881.*
   Note.—Also a copy in Department of State.

**1884.** Planos de comunicaciones de la provincias de la isla de Cuba con otros datos relativos al ramo de correos par el sub-inspector Du. Sebastian Acosta Quintana. title. 5 maps & 5 tables. fold. sq. 18°. Habana, J. Menéndez & brothers, 1884.

**1886.** Island of Cuba. Cape San Antonia to longitude 76° west with adjacent part of Great Bahama bank. Compiled from the latest british and spanish charts. 1885. Ed. of Aug. 1886. 24x43. Washington, 1886.
   [*United States. Navy Department. Hydrographic office. Chart no. 947.*]

**1894.** Mapa de la isla de Cuba, por el doctor Manuel Pruna Santa Cruz. Habana, 1894. 9½x24. Habana, Castro, Fernandes & co., 1894.

**1896.** The island of Cuba. 2 sheets, each 29x42. Washington, 1896.
   [*In United States. Navy department. Hydrographic office.*]
   Note.—Copy in Department of State.

**1896.** Cuba en 1896. Publicado por la imprenta "America." 14x19. New York, G. W. & C. B. Colton & co. 1896.
   [*In Pierra (Fidel G.) Cuba. 8°. New York, S. Figueroa, 1896.*]

**1897.** Map and history of Cuba from the latest and best authorities. By E. Hannaford, 32 p. p. 1 fold. map. 18°. Springfield, O; Mast, Crowell & Kirkpatrick, 1897.

**1897.** Mapa de la isla de Cuba. Col. 18x34. Philadelphia, J. L. Smith, 1897.

**1897.** Mapa del teatro de la guerra de Cuba comprendiendo la mitad oriental de la isla desde Santa Clara hasta la punta Maysi. Dibujado por d. José Rindavets y Cudury segun los datos más completos publicados hasta el dia y editado par la empresa de la Ilustracion Española y Americana. 2 sheets, each 19x31. Madrid, Rivadeneyra [1897].

**N. D.** Carta geò-typográfica de la isla de Cuba. Por el auditor hone. de marina d. Estében Pichardo. 7 sheets, each 27x37. Habana, grabado par Martin [n. d.].

**N. D.** Isla de Cuba n. d. n. p. 20x51. Colored map done by hand. 51¼x20¼.
*In Deposito. De la Guerra (original text).*
Note.—In Department of State.

## HAVANA.

**1615-1679.** Plano manuscrito de la ciudad de la Habana en 1615, que se halla en las carteras del depósito de la marina en Paris. [And] Plano manuscrito con-servado en el mismo depósito, y que lleva por leyenda: La Havane en 1679, envoyó par M. le C. d'Estrées, snivant sa lettre de 10 octobre 1679, à Brest.
[*In Sagra (Ramón de la). Historia física, política y natural de la isla de Cuba. fol. Paris, A. Bertrand, 1842. vol. 2, pl. 7.*]

**1695.** Plano manuscrito de la ciudad y puerto de la Habana, sin fecha ni nombre de autor. Puesto que representa la murilla de la fortificacion como concluida, debe ser el mapa posterior al año de 1695. 13x8¼.
[*In Sagra (Ramón de la). Historia física, política y natural de la Isla de Cuba. fol. Paris, A. Bertrand, 1842. vol. 2, pl. 8.*]

**17—.** A new and correct chart of the harbour of Havana on the island of Cuba, with a plan of ye city & from actual survey by capt. James Phelps. I. Mynde sc. 17x21½. London, W. Mount & T. Page, (17—).
[American maps. v. 2, no. 5.]

**17—.** Plan of the city & harbour, of the Havannah, together with the adjacent forts & batteries. ms. (anon.) col. 8x14. (n. p. 17—.)

**1722.** Baye et ville de la Havana on de S. Christoval. 8x13.
[*In Coreal (François). Voyages. 16°. Amsterdam, 1722. v. 1, facing p. 8.*]

**1743-44.** A plan of the harbour, city, and forts of Havana, on the north side of the island of Cuba. W. H. Toms, engraver. col. 11x14½. Holbourn, W. H. Toms, 1743-44.

**176-.** Plan of the city and harbour of the Havana. T. Jefferys, sculp. 8x10½. (London, 176-.)

**1762.** An exact plan of the city, fortifications & harbour of Havana in the island of Cuba, from an original drawing taken on the spot. (anon.) 11½x14.
[London.] J. Hinton, [1762].
[*In Universal (The) magazine. 8°. J. Hinton, 1762. v. 30. May 1762. facing p. 225.*]

**1762.** A plan of the siege of the Havana, drawn by an officer on the spot. 1762. 8½x14.
[*In Authentic (An) journal of the siege of the Havana. By an officer. [anon.] 16°. London, for T. Jefferys, 1762.*]

**1762.** Plans of the city and harbour of Havana. (anon.) each 4½x7½.
[*In London (The) magazine. 8°. London, for R. Baldwin, (1762). v. 31. May 1762. facing p. 280.*]

**1763.** A view of the Moor's castle near the Havana, whilst besieged by us. (anon.) 4x6. (London, 1763.)
[*In London (The) magazine. 8°. London, for R. Baldwin (1763). v. 32. april 1763. facing pp. 184.*]

**1768.** Plan of the city and harbour of Havana. (anon.)

    [*In Jefferys (Thomas engraver) A general topography of North America and the West Indies. fol. London, for R. Sayer and T. Jefferys, 1768. no. 80.*]

**1772.** Attack of the Havana. Engrav'd by J. Lodge. 28¼x15.

    [*In Mante (Thomas). The history of the late war in North America. 4°. London, 1772. p. 397.*]

**1778.** Plano della citta, porto dell' Havana. 8x10.

    [*In Atlante dell' America. (anon.) fol. Livorno, 1778. no. 19.*]

**1798.** Plan of the city of the Havana surveyed by Don Joseph Del Rio, captain in the spanish navy, 1798. (The meridian and scale have been corrected by commander E Barnett, 1844.) 16x20¼.

    [*Great Britain. Admiralty Chart no. 414.*]

**1801.** Havana. 6x5.

    [*In Luffman (John) Select plans of the principal cities, harbours, forts, etc., in the world. sm. 4°. London, 1801. v. 2.*]

**1818.** Plan of the city and harbour of Havana. (&) Plan of the bay of Matanzas, on the north side of Cuba.

    [*In Whittle (J.) and Laurie (H. R.) The West India atlas. fol. London, J. Whittle and R. H. Laurie, 1818. no. 49.*]

**1842.** Plano de la ciudad y del puerto de la Habana. 8¾x14.

    [*In Sagra (Ramón de la). Historia física política y natural de la isla de Cuba. fol. Paris, A. Bertrand, 1842. vol. 2, pl. 10.*]

**1846.** Havana. 1. Situation of h.m's ship "Romney" in the harbour. 2. Situation of the barricoon "Noria" offered by the capt. gen. in place of the Romney. 11x14.

    [*In Great Britain. Parliament. Accounts and papers. 1846. v. 50. p. 422.*]

**1858.** West Indies. Cuba. Havana surveyed by comodore D. Antonio de Arévalo and lieut's. D. Eduardo Failde & D. Manuel Costilla of the spanish navy 1854. Copied from the Chart published at Madrid in 1855. 24x37. London, admiralty. 1858.

    [*Great Britain. Admiralty Chart no. 414.*]

**1879.** Plano de la ciudad y puerto de la Habana segun los trabajos españoles más recientes. 25x39. Madrid, direccion de hidrografia, 1879.

**1882.** West Indies. Cuba. Havana harbour. From the latest surveys published by the spanish government in 1879. Corrected to 1887. 25x38. London, admiralty. 1882.

    [*Great Britain. Admiralty Chart no. 414.*]

## PORTO RICO.

**1719.** Carte topographique de l'ile Saint Jean de Puertorico et de l'ile de Bieque avec leurs divisions, par don Tonias Lopez, géographe des domains de la majesté, membre de diverses académies. Madrid 1719. Avec quelques additions par m. Ledru. Paris, 1810. gravée par J. B. Tardieu, 14x28.

    [*In Ledru (A. P.) Voyage aux îles de Ténériffe. [etc.] 8°. Paris, 1810. v. 2.*]

**1740.** A survey of the west road of Portorico named by the Spaniards Aguada Nueva or New Watering place. Taken by order of Admiral Torres, in 1740 (&) A plan of the forts and harbour of San Juan de Portorico. (anon. London, Laurie & Whittle, n. d.)

    [*In Whittle (J.) and Laurie (W. H.) The West India atlas. fol. London, J. Whittle & W. H. Laurie, 1818. no. 57.*]

**1768.** Plan of the Aguada Nueva de Puerto Rico. [By F. M. Coli, anon.]
[*In Jefferys (Thomas engraver). A general topography of North America and the West Indies. fol. London, for R. Sayer & T. Jefferys, 1768. no. 91a.*]

**1768.** Plan of the town and harbour of San Juan de Puerto Rico. [By le sieur Bully.]
[*In Jefferys (Thomas engraver). A general topography of North America and the West Indies. fol. London, for R. Sayer & T. Jefferys, 1768. no. 90.*]

**1769.** De hoofdstad en haven van't eiland Porto Roco in de Westindien. 7x10.
[*In Hedendaagche historie of tegenwordige staat van Amerika. [anon.] 8°. Te Amsterdam, I. Tirion, 1769. v. 3, p. 173.*]

**1791.** San Juan de Porto Rico. West Indies. Mapa topográfico de la isla de San Juan de Puertorico, y la de Bieque, con la division de sus partidos. Por don Thomas Lopez. 1791. col. fold. 14x29. [Madrid 1791.]

**1822.** Geographical, statistical, and historical map of Porto Rico and the Virgin islands. Drawn by E. Lucas. 10½x17.
[*In Complete (A.) historical, chronological and geographical american atlas. fol. Philadelphia, H. C. Carey & I. Lea, 1822. no. 43.*]

**1836.** Plano topográfico de la isla de Sn. Juan Bautista de Puerto Rico, año 1836. N. Currier's lith. Bancroft & Holley direxit. 21x32. [New York 1836.]

**1842.** Carta particular esférica y corográfica de la isla de Puerto Rico y las adyacentes que á la misma pertenecen Vieques, Culobra, Culebrita, Caja de Muertos, Mona, Monito y Desecheo. Publicada por la direccion de hidrografía y presentada a s. m. y al regente del reyno por el exmo señor secretario de estado y del despacho de la marina, comercio y gobernacion de ultramar Mariscal de Campo don Andrés García Camba. Madrid, año 1842. 14x21.

**1851.** Posesiones de América. Isla de Puerto Rico. Por el teniente coronel capitan de ingenieros D. Francisco Coello. Las notas estadísticas ó históricas han sido escritas. Por D. Pascual Madoz. 33x44. Madrid, J. Noguerra, 1851.
NOTE.—At top of sheet "Diccionario-geográfico-estatistico histórico. Atlas de España, sus posesiones de ultramar." Copy in Department of State.

**1855.** The Virgin islands. 26x37. London, J. Imray & son, 1855.
NOTE.—Contains the east part of Porto Rico.

**1861.** Carte de l'ile de Saint Jean de Puerto-Rico. Gravó chez Erhard. 7x10¼.
[*In Société de géographie. Bulletin 5° série. 1861, juillet-dec. 8°. Paris, Arthus-Bertrand, 1861. v. 2, at end.*]

**1864.** Nuevo mapa topográfico de la isla de Puerto Rico. Con planos extensos de los principales puertos y notas estadísticas compiladas de datas oficiales 40x58. Nueva York, J. H. Colton. 1864.
Contains Mapa de las Antillas, contoros de Ponce. Mapa de los contornos de S. Juan de Puerto Rico. Mapa de las yslas de Cuba y Santo Domingo y Jamaica. Plano de S. Juan de Puerto Rico. Mapa de la isla Culebra y Vieques y canales entre ellas y Puerto Rico, etc.
NOTE.—Copy in Department of State.

**1873.** Puerto Rico. From the latest surveys, corrected to 1873. 25x45. Washington, 1873.
[*United States. Navy Department. Hydrographic Office. Chart no. 538.*]

S. Doc. 161——4

## WEST INDIES.

**1492.** Créquis de una parte de los archipiélagos de Bahama y Antillas, para elucidar
principalmente las cuestiones de cuales sean la verdadera Guanahani de
Colon i el puerto de la isla de Cuba, en que primero recaló. 11½x18½.
[*In Varhagan (F. A.) La verdadera Guanhani de Colon. 8º. Santiago. 1864.*]

**1605.** Residvm continentis cvm adiacentibus insvlis. 9x11.
[*In Wytfliet (Cornelius) and others. Histoire vniverselle des Indes. fol. Douay,
F. Fabri, 1605. facing p. 97.*]

**1630.** Insula Iamaica. Ins. S. Ioannis. I. S. Margareta cum confinus, Cuba
insula. Hispañiola insula. Havana. 14x19.
[*In Mercator (Gerhard). Atlas. Ed. 10a. Amsterdami, sumptibus, H. Hondij,
1630. p. 387.*]

**1638.** Insvlæ Americanæ in oceano septrionali, cum terris adiacentibus. 15x20½.
Amsterdami, apud Ioannem Ianssonium.
[*Inserted in Linschoten (Jan Huyghen van). Description de l'Amérique. fol.
A. Amsterdam, E. Cloppenburch, 1638. With his Histoire de la navigation.*]

**1653.** Insulæ Americanæ in oceano septentrionali, cum terris adiacentibus Amstel-
odami, apud Ioannem Ianssonium. 14½x20½.
[*In Jansson (Jan.). Neuro atlas. fol. Amsterdam, J. Jansson, 1653. v. 2.*]

**1656.** Les isles Antilles, etc., entre lesquelles sont les Lvcayes, et les Caribes. Par
N. Sanson. 15½x22. Paris, l'authcur, 1656.
[*In Cappel (Jacques). Cartes recueillics en un tome, en 1679. fol. [n. p. 1679.]
no. 119.*]

**1657.** Les isles Antilles, etc., entre lesquelles sont les Lucayes, et les Caribes. Par
N. Sanson, 1657. 8½x12.
[*In his L'Amérique en plvsievrs cartes. 4º. Paris, l'avtherr, 1657. no. 7.*]

**1667.** Canibalis insvlæ. 16½x20½.
[*In Blaauw (W. J.) and Blaauw (Jan). Le grand atlas, ov cosmographie Bla-
viane, contenant l'Amérique. fol. Amsterdam, J. Blaeu, 1667. v. 12, bet. pp.
95-96.*]

**1667.** Insvlæ Americanæ in oceano Septentrionali, cum terris adiacentibus. 15x20½.
[*In Blaauw (W. J.) and Blaauw (Jan). Le grand atlas, ov cosmographie Bla-
viane, contenant l'Amérique. fol. Amsterdam, J. Blaeu, 1667. v. 12, bet. pp.
83-84.*]

**1675.** A chart of the Caribe islands. By John Seller. 17x21.
[*In his Atlas maritimus, or the sea atlas. fol. London, J. Darby, for the author,
1675. no. 45.*]

**1675.** A chart of the West Indies, from cape Cod to the river Oronoque. By John
Seller. 17x23½.
[*In his Atlas maritimus, or the sea atlas. fol. London, J. Darby, for the
author, 1675. no. 40.*]

**1675.** A chart of the West Indies from cape Cod to the river Oronoque. By J. Sel-
ler. 16x20½.
[*London, 1675.*]
[*American maps. v. 4, no. 10.*]

**1675.** Het eerste deel van het brandende veen, verlichtende geheel West Indien.
Door Arent Roggeveen. Ill. title. 5 p. l., 62 pp., 32 col. maps. fol.
l'Amsterdam, P. Goos, (1675.)

**1675.** A general chart of the West India. By John Seller. 17x21½.
    *[In his Atlas maritimus, or the sea atlas. fol. London, J. Darby, for the author, 1675. no. 38.]*

**1676.** A map of Jamaica. (&) Barbados. 15x21.
    *[In Speed (John) The theatre of the empire of Gt. Britaine. New ed. fol. London, T. Basset, 1676. between pp. 47-48.]*

**1680.** A chart of the Caribe islands. By John Thornton. 17½x21½.
    *(London, ab. 1680.)*
    *[American maps. v. 4, no. 23.]*

**1695-97.** Isole Antili, la Cuba, e la Spagnuola. 10x17.
    *[In Coronelli (Vincenzo.) Atlante Veneto. fol. Venetia, 1695-97. v. 2, pt. 2. bet. pp. 160-161.]*

**1705-20.** Carte des Antilles françoises et des isles voisines. 19x12½.
    *[In Chatelain (H. A.) Atlas historique. [anon.] fol. Amsterdam, 1705-20. v. 6, p. 154.]*

**171-.** A chart of ye West Indies or the islands of America in the North sea, &c. Being ye present seat of war. By Herman Moll. 11x13.
    *[London] for T. Bowles and J. Bowles, (171-.)*

**1715.** A map of the West Indies or the islands of America in the North sea, with ye adjacent countries; explaining what belongs to Spain, England, France, Holland, &c. also ye trade winds, and ye several tracts made by ye galeons and flota from place to place. By Herman Moll. 33x40.
    *[London] for T. Bowles & J. Bowles, (1715?)*
    *[American maps. v. 1, no. 13.]*

**1715-20.** Moll (Herman). A map of the West Indies, or the islands of America in the North sea; with ye adjacent countries; explaining which belongs to Spain, (etc.). 24x38.
    *[In his The world described. fol. London, 1715-20. no. 10.]*

**1717.** Carte des Antilles françoises et des isles voisines. Dressée sur les mémoires manuscrits de mr. Petit, et sur quelques observations. Par Guillaume Del'isle. 15x25. Paris, l'auteur, 1717.
    *[American maps, v. 1, no. 11; v. 2, no. 11.]*

**1721.** A new map of the English empire in the ocean of America, or West Indies. Revis'd by I. Senex. 20x23.
    *[In New general atlas. (anon.) fol. London, for D. Browne, 1721. facing p. 186.]*

**1731.** Carte des isles de l'Amérique et de plusieurs pays de terre ferme situés au devant de ces isles & autour du golfe de Mexique. Par le sr. d'Anville. 1731. 12x17.
    *[In his Atlas général. fol. Paris, 1727-80. no. 36.]*

**1733.** Carte des Antilles françoises et des isles voisines, dressée sur les mémoires manuscrits de mr. Petit, et sur quelques observations. Par Guillaume De l'Isle. 17½x23. Amsterdam, J. Cóvens & C. Mortier, (1733).
    *[In his Atlas nouveau. fol. Amsterdam, J. Covens & C. Mortier, (1741)? v. 2. no. 42.]*
    NOTE.—This map is also found in the edition of 1733.

**1752.** An accurate map of the West Indies. By Eman. Bowen. 13½x16½.
    *[In his A complete atlas. fol. London, for W. Innys, (etc.) 1752. no. 57.]*

**1755.** A new and accurate map of the West Indies and the adjacent parts of North and South American. R. W. Scalc, sculp. 10½x15.
  [*In Universal (The) magazine. 8°. London, J. Hinton, 1755. v. 17, p. 241.*]

**1758.** Déscription géographique des illes Antilles possedées par les anglois. Par le sr. Bellin. 1758. XII, 171 pp., 13 maps. 4°. Paris, Didot, 1758.

**1758.** A new and correct chart of the trading part of the West Indies. 18x28.
  [*In English (The) pilot. 4th book. (anon.) fol. London, for W. & J. Mount, 1758. p. 58.*]

**1758.** A new general chart of the West Indies. 18x22½.
  [*In English (The) pilot. 4th book. (anon.) fol. London, for W. & J. Mount, 1758. p. 3.*]

**1759.** Dominia anglorum in præcipius insulis Americæ ut sunt insula S. Christophori, Antegoa, Iamaica, Barbados nec non insulæ Bermudes vel Sommers dictæ, singulari mappa omnia exhibita et edita ab Homanniauis heredibu . --Die englische colonie--lænder auf den insuln von America.
  [*In Homann (J. B.) Atlas geographicus maior. fol. Norimbergæ, Homannianis heredibus, 1759. v. 1. no. 142.*]

**1759.** Mappa geographica, complectens 1. Indiæ Occidentalis partem mediam circvm Isthmvm Panamensem. 2. Ipsumq₃ isthmum. 3. Ichnographiam præcipuorum locorum & portuum ad has terras pertinentium. Desumeta omnia ex historia insula. S. Dominici & pro præsenti statu belli, quod est 1740 inter Anglos & Hispanos exortum, luci publicæ tradita ad Homannianis heredibus. 19x22.
  [*In Homann (J. B.) Atlas geographicus maior. fol. Norimbergæ, Homannianis heredibus, 1759. v. 1. no. 144.*]

**1760.** The West Indies: exhibiting the english, french, spanish, dutch, and danish settlements. 18x18.
  [*In Jefferys (Thomas) The natural and civil history of the french dominion in N. & S. America. fol. London, 1760. pt. 2, facing p. 1.*]

**1762.** An accurate map of the West Indies. Engraved by A. Bell. 7x9½.
  [*In Scots (The) magazine. 1762. 8°. Edinburgh, W. Sands, (etc.). 1762. v. 2, p. 557.*]

**1762.** An accurate map of the british, french, & spanish settlements in Nth. America and the West Indies, as stipulated by the preliminary articles of peace signed at Fontainebleau, by the ministers of Great Britain, France, & Spain, nov. 3, 1762. J. Gibson, sculp. (anon.) 13x11. (n. p. 1762?)

**1762.** A new and correct map of the American islands, now called the West Indies, with the whole coast of the neighbouring continent. By Thos. Kitchin. 11x14.
  [*In London (The) magazine. 8°. London, for R. Baldwin. (1762). v. 31. sept. 1762. facing p. 464.*]

**1762.** A new and correct map of the West Indies. J. Gibson, sculp. (anon.) 11x13½.
  [*In American (The) gazetteer. [anon.] 12°. London, for A. Millar, 1762. v. 3.*]

**1768.** A new chart of the West Indies, drawn from the best spanish maps, and regulated by astronomical observations. [anon.]
  [*In Jefferys (Thomas, engraver). A general topography of North America and the West Indies. fol. London, for R. Sayer & T. Jefferys, 1768. no. 72.*]

**1766.** Chart of the Atlantic ocean, with the british, french, & spanish settlements in North America, and the West Indies; as also on the coast of Africa. By Thos. Jefferys.
[*In Jefferys (Thomas, engraver). A general topography of North America and the West Indies. fol. London, for R. Sayer & T. Jefferys, 1768. no. 15.*]

**1767.** Algemeene kaart van de West-Indische eilander. 14x17½.
[*In Hedendaagsche historie of tegenwoordige staat van Amerika. [anon.] 8°. Te Amsterdam, I. Tirion, 1767. v. 3, facing p, 1.*]

**1768.** The West Indies; exhibiting the english, french, spanish, dutch, and danish settlements. Collected from the best authorities by Thomas Jefferys.
[*In Jefferys (T. engraver). A general topography of North America and the West Indies. fol. London, for R. Sayer & T. Jefferys, 1768. nos. 70–71.*]

**1769.** Algemeene kaart van de West-indische eilanden. 14x17½. Te Amsterdam, I. Tirion (1769).
[*In Hedendaagsche historie of tegenwoordige staat van Amerika. [anon.] 8°. Te Amsterdam, I. Tirion, 1769. v. 3, p. 1.*]

**1771.** The West India pilot. By capt. Joseph Smith Speer. 4 p. l., 67 pp., 26 maps. fol. London, for the author, 1771.

**1774.** Chart of the West Indies, by Joseph Smith Speer. Thos. Bowen sculp. col. 28x46. [London] capt. Speer, 1774.
[*American maps. v. 2. no. 33.*]

**1774.** A compleat map of the West Indies, containing the coasts of Florida, Louisiana, New Spain, and Terra Firma; with all the islands. By Samuel Dunn. 12x17½. London, for R. Sayer, 1774.
[*In Sayer (Robert) and Bennett (John), editors. The american military pocket atlas. [anon.] 8°. London, for R. Sayer & J. Bennett, [1776]. no. 1.*]

**1775.** Jefferys (Thomas). The West-India atlas: or, a compendius description of the West Indies. fol. London, for R. Sayer & J. Bennett, 1775.

**1777.** A new and correct map of North America, with the West India Islands. Laid down according to the latest surveys and corrected from the original materials of govern. Pownall, 1777. London, for R. Sayer & J. Bennett, 1777.
[*In Faden (William, editor). The North American atlas. fol. London, for W. Faden, 1777. nos. 1–2.*]

**1777.** A new and correct map of North America, with the West India islands. Wherein are particularly distinguished the several provinces and colonies which compose the british empire. Laid down according to the latest surveys, and corrected from the original materials of govern. Pownall, 1777. London, for R. Sayer & J. Bennett, 1777.
[*In Jefferys (T.) and others The American atlas. fol. London, R. Sayer & J. Bennett, 1776. nos. 5–6.*]

**1777.** West Indien. 7x15.
[*In Schlözer (A. L.) Neue erdbeschreibung der ganz Amerika. 16°. Gothingen, 1777.*]

**1778.** A new chart of the West Indian islands; as they are possessed by the european powers; drawn from the most recent authorities. (anon.) fold. 19x23. [London] for R. Sayer & J. Bennett, 1778.

**1778.** Nuovo e corretta carta dell' Indie Occidentali. 10½x13.
[*In Atlante dell' America. [anon.] fol. Livorno, 1778. no. 17.*]

**1798.** Map of the european settlements in the West Indies. By Thos. Kitchin. 6¼x10¼.

[*In Raynal (G. T. F.) A philosophical and political history* [etc.]. 12º. *Dublin, 1779. v. 4.*]

NOTE.—Also in second edition, 1798.

**1780.** West Indies, with the harbour and fort of Omoa. From the best authorities. (anon.) 11¼x25.

[*In Political (The) magazine.* 8º. *London, for J. Bew, (1780). v. 1, march 1780, facing p. 179.*]

**1782.** West Indien. Samuel Vitus Dorn sc. 7x14¼.

[*In Geschichte der kriege in und ausser Europa.* [anon.] 4º. *Nürnbrg, G. Raspé, 1782. 25 theil.*]

**1783.** Bowles (Carington). Bowles' new map of North America and the West Indies, exhibiting the british empire therein with the limits and boundaries of the United States. As also, the french and other european states. The whole compiled from the best surveys and authentic memoirs which have appeared to the present year 1783. col. 39x45. fold. 8º. London, C. Bowles, 1783.

**1783.** Jefferys (Thomas). The West India atlas. fol. London, for R. Sayer & J. Bennett, 1783.

**1784.** A chart of the Antilles, or Charibee, or Caribs islands, with the Virgin isles, by L. S. De La Rochette. 1784. W. Palmer sculp. 18x20. London, W. Faden, 1784.

**1786.** A compleat map of the West Indies containing the coasts of Florida, and Terra Firma; with all the islands. By Samuel Dunn. 12x17¼. London, for R. Sayer, 1786.

[*In Dunn (Samuel). A new atlas of the mundane system. 3d ed. fol. London, Laurie & Whittle, (1786–89). Map 41.*]

**1794.** An accurate map of the West Indies. W. Harrison sculp. 8x10. London, R. Wilkinson, 1794.

[*In Wilkinson (Robert). A general atlas. fol. London, 1800.*]

**1794.** Jefferys (Thomas). The West-India atlas. fol. London, for R. Sayer, 1794.

**1796.** A chart of the West Indies, from the latest marine journals and surveys. W. Barker sculp. (anon.) 11x16.

[*In Carey (Mathew). Carey's american atlas. fol. Philadelphia, M. Carey, 1796. no. 21.*]

**1796.** An accurate map of the West Indies with the adjacent coast of America. 1796. D. Martin sculp. 14x17¼.

[*In American (The) atlas. fol. New York, J. Reid, 1796. no. 20.*]

**1797.** West Indies, from the best authorities. 7¼x12¼.

[*In Morse (Jedidiah). The american gazetteer. 8º. Boston, 1797.*]

**1800.** The West Indies and gulf of Mexico, from the latest discoveries and best observations. Jno. Lodge sculp. 9x14.

[*In Russell (William). The history of America. 4º. London, for Walker, 1800. v. 1, p. 517.*]

**1803.** A new map of the West India isles. By John Cary. col. 18x20. London, J. Cary, 1803.

[*In Cary (John). Cary's new universal atlas. fol. London, J. Cary, 1808. no. 58.*]

**1804.** West Indies, from the best authorities. Grilbey sc. 7x12.

[*In Morse (Jedidiah). The american gazetteer. 2d ed. 8°. Charlestown, 1804.*]

**1809.** Portulano de la America Septentrional. Construido en la direccion de los trabajos hydrográficos. 2 p. l., 16, 46, 34, 16, 9 maps obl. fol. Madrid, 1809. aumentado y corregido, en 1818.

**1810.** Edwards (Bryan). A new atlas of the british West Indies. Engraved to accompany the Phila. ed. of Edward's History of the West Indies. Title. 11 maps. 4°. Charleston, E. Morford, (etc.). 1810.

NOTE.—Maps also found in plates, etc., to other edition.

**1811.** West Indies, drawn from the best authorities by J. Russell. 14x18½.

[*In Guthrie (Wm.). A system of modern geography. 7th ed. 8°. London, 1811. p. 934.*]

**1810-16.** Chart of the West Indies and Spanish dominions in North America. By A. Arrowsmith. 1803. Additions to 1810-1816. 2 sheets.

[*In Arrowsmith (Aaron). Atlas to Thompson's Alcedo. fol. London. G. Smeeton, 1816. maps 12-13.*]

**1817.** West Indies. Engraved by Sy. Hall. 8x10. Edinburgh, A. Constable & co., 1817.

[*In Arrowsmith (Aaron). A new general atlas. 4°. Edinburgh, A. Constable & co., 1817. no. 52.*]

**1817.** Laurie & Whittle's new chart of the Caribbee or West India islands, from Porto-Rico to Trinidad inclusive; with the coasts of the Spanish Main then to Guayra. Improved by various emendations and additions, from the chart constructed under the orders of the spanish government, by don Cosme Churruca, and don Joaquin Franco. Fidalgo, John Purdy delint. 3d ed. 1817. London, R. Laurie & J. Whittle, 1810 (1817).

[*In Whittle (J.) and Laurie (R. H.). The West India atlas. fol. London, J. Whittle & R. H. Laurie, 1818. nos. 9-10.*]

**1818.** A new chart of the West Indies, gulf of Mexico and northern provinces of South America; compiled from the most recent spanish and other surveys by Joseph Dession. Improved with additions to 1818. London, J. Whittle & R. H. Laurie, 1813 (1818).

[*In Whittle (J.) and Laurie (R. H.). The West India atlas. fol. London, J. Whittle & R. H. Laurie, 1818. nos. 7-8.*]

**1818.** Purdy (John) Dession (Joseph) and Jefferys (Thomas). The West India atlas. fol. J. Whittle & R. H. Laurie, 1818.

**1818.** Riley (Isaac, publisher). A new atlas of the West India islands. title. 10 maps. 4°. Philadelphia, I. Riley, 1818.

**1818.** West Indies. 20x27.

[*In Pinkerton (John). A modern atlas. fol. Philadelphia, T. Dobson, 1818. no. 47.*]

**1818.** The West-India atlas: comprehending a complete collection of accurate charts of the navigation of the West Indies and gulf of Mexico, etc. [By James Whittle and Richard Holmes Laurie.] fol. London, J. Whittle & R. H. Laurie, 1818.

**1822.** Carey (H. C.) and Lea (I.). A complete historical, chronological, and geographical american atlas, being a guide to the history of North and South America and the West Indies, etc. According to the plan of Le Sage's atlas and intended as a companion to Lavoisne. 3 p. l.; 67 sheets, incl. 46 maps. fol. Philadeldhia, H. C. Carey & I. Lea, 1822.

**1827.** Carey (H. C.) & Lea (I.). A complete historical, chronological, and geographical american atlas, being a guide to the history of North and South
America, and the West Indies. 3d ed. · 3 p. 1, 53 sheets. fol. Philadelphia, H. C. Carey & I. Lea, 1827.

**1839.** Map of the West India & Bahama islands, with the adjacent coasts of Yuca-
tan, Honduras, Colombia, &c. 20x29.
*[In Tanner (Henry S.). A new american atlas. fol. Philadelphia, H. S.
Tanner, 1839.]*

**1842.** Map of the Leeward islands; comprising Antigua, Montserrat, Barbuda, St.
Christopher, Nevis, Anguilla, Virgin islands & Dominica. By John
Arrowsmith. 18x23½. London, J. Arrowsmith, 1842.
*[In his The London atlas of universal geography. fol. London, J. Arrow-
smith, 1842-(1850). no. (65).]*

**1842.** Map of the Windward islands; comprising Barbados, St. Vincent, Grenada,
Tobago, St. Lucia & Trinidad. By John Arrowsmith. 18½x24. London,
J. Arrowsmith, 1842.
*[In his The London atlas of universal geography. fol. London, J. Arrowsmith,
1842-1850. no. 66.]*

**1847.** West Indies. By J. Arrowsmith. 18½x24. London, J. Arrowsmith, 1847.
*[In his The London atlas of universal geography. fol. London, J. Arrowsmith,
1842-(1850). no. 45.]*

**1850.** West India islands, etc. [Showing lights and light houses.] 12½x14.
*[In Great Britain. Parliament. Accounts and papers. 1850. v. 53.]*

**1854.** Map of the West Indies & Bahama Islands with the adjacent coasts of Yuca-
tan, Honduras, Caracas, &c. By James Wyld. 11x30½. London, J.
Wyld, 1851.
*[In Wyld (James). A new general atlas. fol. London, (1854).]*

**1854.** West Indies. Drawn & engraved by J. Dower. 13x16.
*[In Teesdale (Henry) & co. A new general atlas. fol. London, (1854). Map
39.]*

**1857.** West Indies. By Sidney Hall. 16½x20. London, Longman & co. [1857.]
*[In Hall (Sidney). A new general atlas. fol. London, 1857, no. 47.]*

**1858.** H. Kiepert's karte des nördlichen tropischen America.—A new map of tropical America north of the equator, comprising the West Indies, Central
America, Mexico, New Granada, and Venezuela. col. 38x63. fold. obl.
4°. Berlin, D. Reimer, 1858.

**1861.** Colton's map of the United States, Mexico, the West Indies, &c., 1861. col.
30x37. fold. 18°. New York, J. H. Colton & co., [1861.]

**1862.** Colton's new map of the West Indies, showing also part of Central America,
the U. S. of Colombia, Venezuela, etc. 38x56. New York, J. H. Colton,
1862.

**1864.** Johnson (A. J.). Johnson's West Indies. 14x21. [New York] Johnson &
Ward, (1864).

**1874.** Case's map of the United States, British provinces, Mexico and part of the
West Indies. col. 60x70. Hartford, O. D. Case & co., 1874.

**1874.** The granger's map of the United States, British provinces, West Indies, Mexico and Central America. [By Gaylord Watson.] 38x50. Chicago, Watson's Chicago branch, 1874.

**1876.** William's [G. W.] copper-plate map of the United States, Canada, Mexico, Central America, West Indies, etc. col. 63x63. Philadelphia, J. M. Atwood, (1876).

**1876.** West India islands and Caribbean sea. Sheet 1. Comprising Florida strait, Bahama islands, and the Greater Antilles. 1876. 25½x37½. London, admiralty, 1876.

    *[Great Britain, Admiralty.  Chart 761.]*

# APPENDIX.

## A Synoptical Catalogue of Manuscripts in the Library of Congress Relating to Cuba.

Compiled by HERBERT FRIEDENWALD, PH. D.,

*Superintendent, Manuscript Department.*

[All but two of the manuscripts referred to in the following catalogue are to be found in the twelve large folio volumes of "Vernon-Wager Navy Papers," which contain an invaluable mass of unpublished material relating to American Colonial history of the early part of the eighteenth century. The letters VW. have reference to these papers.

The last two manuscripts in the list are to be found in a slender folio entitled "Papers Relating to Havannah." The letters Ch. have reference to this volume.]

**1710** (?). Plan of an attempt on Havanna [September-November, 1710 ?]. Statement of the advantages of that place to Great Britain; a method of capturing it; number of ships and men required.
*7 pp. Fᵒ. VW. I, 39.*

**1726.** Instructions from the King to Vice-Admiral Hosier, St. James's, March 28, 1726. He is to go in search of Spanish galleons; if they are not found at Carthagena he is to proceed to Portobello, or Havanna, or any other Spanish port where he hears they may be. (Copy.)
*15 pp. Fᵒ. VW. I, 10.*

**1726.** Letter from General Hunter, Charlton, November 12, 1726, to Lord Townsend. Advocates an attack on Cuba and describes how best it can be captured.
*4 pp. Fᵒ. VW. I, 12.*

**1726.** Letter from the Duke of Newcastle, London, November 18, 1726, to Vice-Admiral Hosier. Instructions respecting intercepting Spanish galleons at Havana. (Copy.)
*7 pp. Fᵒ. VW. VIII, 20.*

**1729.** Letter of Marque and Reprisal from Don Dionisio Martinez de la Vega (governor of Cuba), Havanna, April 16, 1729, to Don Felix Joseph D'Acosta Furtado Junr. (Copy.)
*3 pp. Fᵒ. VW. III, 48.*

**1732.** Letter from Don Pedro Xemenes (governor of Santiago de Cuba), May 18, 1732, to Hon. Charles Stewart. Expresses friendship and a desire to aid in the suppression of privateers.
*3 pp. Fᵒ. VW. II, 14.*

**1736.** Letter from Leonard Cock to Digby Dent, Santiago de Cuba, November 3, 1736. Affairs and individuals at Santiago.
*2 pp. Fᵒ. VW. VII, 48.*

**1737.** "Observations on the letter from the Havanna dated the 23d Jany., 1737." By Sir Charles Wager. Proposed protection against invasion of Georgia and Carolina by Spanish privateers from Havanna.
*2 pp. Q°. VW. II, 44°.*

**[1737-8 ?]** Memorandum about supplying Havanna with negroes from the Island of Providence (Bahamas).
*2 pp. Q°. VW. II, 52.*

**1738.** List of Spanish ships of war and their disposition, showing 12 at Havanna and 6 others in West Indies. August 24, 1738.
*1p. Q°. VW. III, 7.*

**1738.** List of Spanish ships of war in the West Indies, September 6, 1738. (5 at Havanna, 6 on their way there.)
*2 pp. F°. VW. III, 7ᵇ.*

**[1738 ?]** Memorandum of Sir Charles Wager about Cuba.
*1 p. Q°. VW. II, 37.*

**1739.** Instructions from Vice-Admiral Vernon, Port Royal, Jamaica, January 31, 1739. To Captain Boscawen, he is to prey on Spanish vessels entering Havanna. (Copy.)
*3 pp. F°. VW. X, 71.*

**1739.** Letter from J. Hamilton, London, May 14, 1739, to Sir Charles Wager. Encloses proposal for taking Cuba.
*1 p. Q°. VW. III, 13ᵃ.*

**1739.** Plan of J. Hamilton for taking Cuba. London, May 14, 1739.
*2 pp. F°. VW. III, 13ᵇ.*

**1739.** Letter from Sir Herbert Jassell, London, October 24, 1739, to Sir Charles Wager. Has been for seven years a resident of Havanna and is familiar with the strength of its garrison; an attack on the island should be made in force.
*2 pp. F°. VW. III, 27.*

**[1739 ?]** "Proposal to take the Island of Cuba with very little Expence to England by a Force rais'd in the American Colonies."
*4 pp. F°. VW. III, 14.*

**1740.** Minutes of a council of war held at Havanna, April 27, 1740, between the Governor of Cuba and sundry other officials. (Translation.)
*7 pp. F°. VW. IV, 18.*

**1740.** Affidavit of Richard Lee [Kingston, Jamaica], September 15, 1740, respecting the privateering expedition of Christopher Edzey to Cuba, and his interference with the Spanish trade from Jamaica.
*3 pp. F°. VW. I, 1ᵇ.*

**1740.** Letter from Don Francisco Carigal de la Vega (governor of Santiago de Cuba) to the Marquis de Larnage (governor of Hispaniola). (Translation.)
*3 pp. F°. VW. V, 15.*

**1740.** Letter same to same. (Copy.) Cuba, November 22, 1740.
*1 p. F°. VW. V, 15ᵃ.*

**1740.** "List of His Majesty's ships under the command of Vice-Admiral Vernon." [London.] December 15, 1740.
*2 pp. F°. VW. XI, 40.*

**[1740?]** (1) Observations, by Sir Charles Wager, on the war in the West Indies.
    *4 pp. F°. VW. IV, 45.*
    (2) Places where the Spaniards may be attacked in Europe and the West Indies.
    *4 pp. F°. Ibid, 45ª.*
    (Memoranda in the handwriting of Sir Charles Wager.)

**[1740?]** Petition of the merchants of Kingston, Jamaica, to Admiral Vernon, praying for his protection against privateers who molest their trade with the Spanish West Indies. (Cuba.)
    *2 pp. F°. WV. I, 1.*

**[1740?]** Petition of merchants of Jamaica to the governor, Edward Trelawney, praying for protection against privateers who molest their trade with the Spanish West Indies. (Cuba.)
    *2 pp. F°. VW. I, 1ª.*

**[1740?]** "Proposal For the Taking of Cuba, by Attacking the Havanna. St. Iago de Cuba, and other Cities and Towns in that Island, and Subjecting the Whole to the King of Great Britain."
    *6 pp. F°. VW. IV, 53.*

**1741.** Letter from Don Rodrigo de Torres y Morales (commander of Spanish squadron), Havana, February 26, 1741, to Marquis de Laruage (governor of Hispaniola). Is prepared for the enemy and expects cooperation. (Translation.)
    *2 pp. F°. VW. V, 21.*

**1741.** Letter from the Marquis de Larnage (governor of Hispaniola), Petit Gouave-San Domingo, March 5, 1741, to Vice-Admiral Vernon. Expresses his determination to preserve a strict neutrality as between Spain and Great Britain; expects to be treated similarly. (In French; copy.)
    *7 pp. F°. VW. V, 22.*

**1741.** Letter from Don Rodrigo de Torres y Morales (commander of Spanish squadron), Havana, March 12, 1741, to the Marquis de Laruage (governor of Hispaniola). (Translation.)
    *2 pp. F°. VW. V, 23.*

**1741.** Letter from Don Francisco de Guemes y Horcasitas (governor of Havana), Havana, March 12, 1741, to the Marquis de Larnage (governor of Hispaniola). Comments on failure of French fleet to cooperate with the Spanish to protect Cuba; the preparations for the defense of Havana. (Translation.
    *3 pp. F°. VW. V, 23ᵇ.*

**1741.** Letter from Marquis de Larnage (governor of Hispaniola), Leogan, March 19, 1741, to Don Francisco Carigal de la Vega (governor of Santiago de Cuba). The movements of the English fleet; effect of the Emperor's death on European affairs. (Translation.)
    *2 pp. F°. VW. V, 24ª.*

**1741.** Council of war held at St. Iago de la Vega (Jamaica), May 26, 1741, between the governor, Edward Trelawney, Vice-Admiral Vernon, and other officers. Determination to attack Santiago de Cuba; dissent of Governor Trelawney from this plan; advises attack on Panama instead. (Copy.)
    *5 pp. F°. VW. VI, 12.*

**1741.** (1) Letter from Vice-Admiral Vernon, Port Royal, Jamaica, May 30, 1741, to Sir Charles Wager. Incloses account of proceedings of council of war of May 26; anticipates being able to move on Cuba by June 10; his plan of procedure. (Autograph, with postscript in Vice-Admiral Vernon's handwriting.)
*12 pp. F°. VW. VI, 14–15.*

(2) The same. Endorsed: "Adm. Vernon. Recd. 2d Sept per the Tonnington."
*12 pp. F°. VW. VI, 16–17.*

**1741.** "Thoughts" of Vice-Admiral Vernon, June 6, 1741, respecting the uses to which the Spanish dominions in America may be put when captured by Great Britain.
*Holograph. 3 pp. F°. VW. VI, 19.*

**1741.** Instructions from Vice-Admiral Vernon, Port Royal, Jamaica, June 13, 1741, to Captain Dent, commander of the "Tilbury." He is to make a special endeavor to discover if the squadron under Don Rodrigo de Torres is as yet at Havanna. (Copy.)
*3 pp. F°. VW. I, 2.*

**1741.** Letter from Vice-Admiral Vernon, Port Royal, Jamaica, June 18, 1741, to Sir Charles Wager. His fleet is almost in readiness to proceed against Cuba.
*5 pp. F°. VW. VI, 21.*

**1762.** Letter of Lieut. Col. A. Monypenny, "Havannah, 15th August, 1762," to [the governor of New York?] Describes the capture of Cuba from the landing near Coxemar Castle, June 7, to the capitulation of Havanna, August 11–14. Indorsed: "Recd. Sept. ye 5th."
*7 pp. F°. Ch. 1.*

**1762.** Orderly book of Lt. Col. Israel Putnam, Havanna, August 25 to October 16, 1762. Putnam was in command of the Connecticut regiment at the siege of Havanna. (Copy.)
*31 pp. F°.*

**1794.** Exports from Havanna, 1777–1780, 1782–1786. A tabulated statement, dated December 27, 1794, of the monetary valuation of 22 articles exported during those years, compiled by Don Antonio de la Paz, "Treasurer of the Custom-House," with explanatory notes upon the customs revenues and the value of Spanish money. Indorsed: "From Mr. A. Dalrymple, 27th Dec'., 1794."
*2 pp. Q°. Ch. 2, 3.*